P9-CBH-532

Pretty Girls

Pretty Girls

a novel by

GARRET WEYR

CROWN PUBLISHERS, INC.
NEW YORK

Grateful acknowledgment is given for permission to reprint lyrics from the following: On page 6, from "What's Love Got To Do With It" by Terri Britten and Graham Lyle. Copyright © 1984 by Myaxe Music Ltd. and Rondor Music Ltd. All rights reserved. Used by permission of Chappell/Intersong Music Group U.S.A. On page 7, from "Carolina in My Mind" by James Taylor. Copyright ©1969, 1971 by Blackwood Music Inc./Country Road Music Ltd. Used by permission of SBK Entertainment World. On page 141, from "I Am Woman," words by Helen Reddy, music by Ray Burton. Copyright © 1971 by Irving Music Inc. and Buggerlugs Music Co. All rights reserved. Used by permission of Almo Music Corp. On page 144, from "Delta Dawn" by Alex Harvey and Larry Collins. Copyright © 1972 by United Artist Music Co., Inc. and April Music, Inc. All rights reserved. Used by permission of SBK Entertainment World. On page 191, from "Ricochet" by David Bowie. Copyright © 1983 by Jones Music America. All rights reserved. Used by permission of the author.

Published by Crown Publishers, Inc., 225 Park Avenue South, New York, New York 10003 and represented in Canada by the Canadian MANDA Group

CROWN is a trademark of Crown Publishers, Inc.
Manufactured in the United States of America
Designed by Lesley Blakeney

Library of Congress Cataloging-in-Publication Data
Weyr, Garret.
Pretty girls.

I. Title.
PS3573.E994P7   1988   813′.54   87-16172

ISBN 0-517-56762-8

10 9 8 7 6 5 4 3 2 1
First Edition

For Mommy and Papa and for my sister Tara

"Oh! Nessim, I have always been so strong.
Has it prevented me from being truly loved?"

LAWRENCE DURRELL, *Justine*

Alex

In her mind, the taxi's tires are beating out a message. Is it twenty pounds—the amount she lost and then regained on doctors' orders last semester when everyone thought she was crazy and anorectic? Is it "Happy Birthday"? Alex twists the ring on her finger—a present that is passed on from mother to daughter on every twentieth birthday. It has been in the family forever, and the responsibility of ownership makes Alex nervous. Alex got it early, as she will turn twenty while at school, away from home.

Maybe it is her mother who has a message, not the tires. Her hair needs retouching, Alex thinks, studying her mother's profile. She'd be so much happier if I were getting on the train to Brown instead of this plane to North Carolina, this foreign strange land where I keep weirding out. They pass a billboard that tells them the next plane to Chicago is at two. LaGuardia is just around the corner.

"Did you pack your vitamins, dear?"

"Yes." Alex thinks it's funny that although she regained the weight, her mother treats her as though she were still ill.

"You think you'll be okay, not living in a dorm this year?"

"Mom, I think not living in a dorm will be the only thing that I can count on being okay."

"I wish you were living with Caroline again. Even Penelope would be good."

"Mom, we've been over that. There's no room in the house Penelope's going to live in, and Caroline can't afford to move out of the dorm. Cristen's okay."

"I hope so. When do the other two get in?"

"I don't know. We're supposed to meet at my house as soon as we pick up our class schedules."

"I hope you like all your courses," Dr. Rust says. "Not the shuttle," she reminds the driver as the airport looms in front of them.

"Look, try... don't worry about me this term. I'll be good."

"Alex, you're always good. I want you to learn that you are also beautiful."

Alex is silent. Her mother leans over to smooth her hair.

"You're always good," Dr. Rust repeats.

They smile at each other, but Alex thinks to herself that being good is part of the problem. Now, if she can just figure out what the problem is.

Penelope

Penelope knows she is being given the once-over by the blue-clad airline attendant, but his voice—saying, "Of course, Ambassador Samms, go right in"—betrays nothing that is in his eyes. They have both been waved into the section marked "Passengers Only." Even now, getting a tighter grip on her bag, dreading the forthcoming five minutes, Penelope has to laugh inwardly at "Ambassador." Her father bought the job with campaign contributions to the current president, and everyone in Paris knows it.

Looking at his grim profile sobers her. Why is it that he

only wants to hassle her when she longs for solitude? She has spent the summer being rude and loud in hopes of some attention, and all it took was a bleeding trip to De Gaulle Airport. Figures.

"Your mother said you might need some of this," Mr. Samms says, handing his daughter two hundred dollars. "The dollar is on the rise, you know."

Suddenly Penelope is tired. She knows there will be no farewell conversation, and she feels cheated. Cheated, but hardly surprised. "Keep it," she says slowly, pushing his hand away. "My stipend is plenty."

"Take it, Penelope," he says, stuffing it into a side pocket of her carry-on. "You can never tell."

"Oh, Daddy, the problem with my life is I can always tell."

"Well, maybe you should do something about that."

"Yes."

Penelope's older sister Anya took razor blades to her wrists (again) and told her father, "I'm so unhappy." Maybe you should do something about that. Carrie ran away with her boyfriend. "I hate it here," she said when the police brought her home. Maybe you should do something about that. The only thing Penelope thinks that she and her sisters need to do anything about is their father. She has been told that he is not that bad. It's hard to tell. What with three brothers and five sisters, Penelope has trouble finding time to spend with her father alone. Right now, though, she wishes he would go away. She needs to go to the duty-free shop and buy Caroline some perfume. "Something sexy, straightforward, and classic" had been the request.

"Yes," Penelope repeats, sitting in one of the red-and-white chairs.

"Would you like a term at the Sorbonne?" he asks suddenly. Penelope vaguely remembers telling him that she did not feel very American, having been born and raised in England and going to America only to visit the estate in Vermont. When she does not answer he goes on, uncomfortable with this gesture of help. "I'm sure I can arrange it. You wouldn't want to come home much, and I know you could have a smashing time."

A smashing time. How Caroline and Alex had roared the first time she said something was "smashing." There is nothing like being the daughter of the American ambassador to Paris and being shipped to English boarding schools to wreak havoc on your vocabulary. What had been smashing? A party? An outfit? She is aware that her father is watching her, but she cannot remember his question, just that it's been a long, long summer.

Caroline

"What's love got to do/Got to do with it?"

Caroline is singing along with Tina—off key. The drive from Colorado to North Carolina is endless, and she has to get her kicks where she can. She was going to stop in Washington and look up her brother's name on the Vietnam memorial in order to beat her parents to it. They are going there next month. She has, however, decided that would be too depressing, and singing with Tina is lifting her spirits, shoving the ghost of Carl from her mind, where it still lives, after all these years. Caroline would like to be like Tina, in endless legs and black leather, but more than that she would like to like herself. Or be Alex. Or Penelope. Without the imperiousness, of course. Caroline does not think she could pull off being imperious. With all the servants that embassies and inherited wealth provide, Penelope was born to it, and Alex can make it sometimes, but Caroline is aware of her limits.

"Too aware of them, darling," Penelope would say. "To have limits is to be limited."

"Whereas you are held back by nothing, not even Daddy?" Alex would answer with more than a touch of sarcasm. Remembering the easy give and take between her friends makes Caroline forget to turn off her brights, and a car honks at her. She switches off the radio.

"In my mind, I'm going to Carolina. / Yes, I'm going to Carolina in my mind," she sings. She thinks she's in the right key. It's hard to tell.

1

Chapel Hill

This year three friends will run to Chapel Hill from, respectively, their past, present, and future. Here, they will both collide and miss one another. Here is the perfect place to do that.

Ostensibly, people come to Chapel Hill for an education. Often, instead of running toward the doors clean notebooks and new books can open, people gather here running from doors they are frightened of slamming.

Although famous only for basketball in most of America, Chapel Hill is *the* university to attend in North Carolina. People instate grow up knowing they will go, have to go, must pray to go. They can spend four years editing the small pretentious literary magazine, which no one reads, or drinking beer in frat court, which everyone does at some point, if only once. They can row crew or organize fasts for hunger. If they study business or studio art, they will have to take a science with a lab. It is required. Whatever people do, chances are they will spend four years thinking it is the only thing to do and the only thing anyone with any sense would do.

Caroline pulls into the circular driveway that surrounds Morrison dorm just in time to see the last freshmen unload their trunks and kiss their parents. She sits in her parked car for a bit, knowing that it will be a while before she can get anywhere near the elevators. Last year she met Alex and her parents in the elevator, unaware that this was the girl she would be rooming with, learning from, loving. Caroline does not have much hope of loving her new roommate and wishes she had the money to live with Alex off campus. Deena Jane King had written to Caroline over the summer on violet monogrammed stationery asking if Caroline would be bringing a quilt, and if so, would it match pink floral print curtains? This may not be such a great year. Caroline has read about sophomore slump. She does not think that a complex carbohydrate diet and an exercise program (the usual prescribed cure) will help her survive another year in this huge red-brick dorm that has not changed one iota since last May.

There is a sameness to Chapel Hill that is both reassuring and terrifying. One sees, year after year, ageing male graduate students who repeatedly pierce their left ears before taking the plunge to the right ones. There are the same high school students who hang out in front of the local greasy spoon ("famous since 1967"), trying to be cool and failing spectacularly. The university *is* Chapel Hill—a town whose sole reason for existence seems to be catering to students. The campus itself is red brick with pretty green trees in strategic places. Each building has an aura and a topic. In Dey they teach languages, and thin men in pleated pants and V-neck sweaters roam the hallways. Math, computer science, and mismatched plaids can be found in Phillips. Greenlaw has no personality. It is the English building, but comparative literature teaches there, as well as political science. People stream all over campus, intent on doing what they believe everyone else is doing—or should be doing. There is the man who hawks the *Durham Morning Herald* to unsuspecting freshmen who think they are getting a bargain. There is the preacher who offers salvation to everyone for no price at all. During the next week, as Caroline walks the campus, trying to organize her class schedule, she wonders if time stopped in Chapel Hill over the summer. She is three months older, but nothing else seems to have aged. The bulletin boards in the Student Union advertise the sameness as well as their wares. Roommates wanted. Iceboxes for sale. Jobs needed. Desperately.

"Darling," Penelope says, "this place is in desperate need of work." She is standing in the doorway of Alex's balcony, surveying the living room, which is haphazardly piled with furniture and unopened boxes. Caroline is sitting in a corner alphabetizing Alex's records.

"You have too much Bowie," she calls.

"There is no such thing," says Alex. She is in the kitchen struggling to get ice out of one of those awful blue plastic trays. She has used a knife, a pot, and a screwdriver. She has not used running water.

Caroline looks up from the records and stares at Penelope, who seems to her an elongated cat in blue shorts and a white top.

"I can't believe you had the nerve," she says. She is referring to Penelope's cropped hair. Normally Penelope has the kind of heavy straight blond hair women murder for; now it is spiky and short with a rattail on the left side.

Penelope shrugs. "Your hair is short."

"Mine has always been this way. It didn't take any kind of dramatics to get it to stand on end."

"Well, all the dramatics were for my father's benefit. I was hoping he would have a fit and at least order me to cut off the braid."

Alex comes out of the kitchen with three cups of Tab, no ice. "I don't care who you did it for. I think it looks great." She puts the cups on an empty bookshelf. "You'll get used to it," she tells Caroline. "God, this place is wrecked. I wish Cristen would do a little work." Cristen is Alex's roommate. She is at her boyfriend's. She is always at her boyfriend's.

Caroline goes back to the records, Penelope continues to lean against the balcony doorframe.

"I would kill or die for a breeze," she says.

Alex lies down on the couch, which arrived yesterday, and stares at the ceiling.

"What's the single most exciting thing everyone did this summer?" She does not wait for an answer. "I think it was telling this group of *carabinieri* to fuck off." Alex spent the summer in Italy and Greece with her best friend from high school. "Celia was so scared of those guys. She kept saying, 'Alex, you, you can't tell someone with a machine gun to fuck off, he just might.' It was classic."

"Why did you?" asks Penelope. "I hear the wop police are stunning."

"Oh, Penelope, you can't get romantically interested in a guy who holds a machine gun in front of his dick and rotates it like a swivel stick."

"So, get *sexually* interested in a guy who does that. He's not looking for romance. Why should you?"

"Penelope, don't be such a cynic." Caroline is on the "C's." "Cher. You have Cher records?" The other girls don't say anything. Alex turns red.

"Alex likes Billy Joel, too," Penelope says. "The most exciting thing I did this summer was get fitted for a diaphragm."

"That was exciting?" Alex sits up. She has not been to the gynecologist for three years, and all she remembers is pain.

"Well, not exactly. I guess it was my father getting the bill that was exciting. They have this whole list of things the doctor can do to you, and they checked off diaphragm fitting just as plain as you please."

"What did he say?" Alex asks.

"'I'm not sure I should be paying for this.' Which, for my dad, is quite a reaction."

"Is it hard to use?" asks Caroline. She has just come off the pill and, though she has no prospects in sight, feels it is best to be prepared.

"It's hard as hell at first. But if you stick your fingers up yourself and figure out the exact path and where the pubic bone is, it's a cinch."

Alex lies back down. "I think the whole thing sounds gross."

Caroline's left foot has fallen asleep. She was going to say that right now was the most exciting part of her summer; that she spent all of it waiting, thinking, hoping, to be back with them, to have the opportunity to see them, talk with them, admire them. She remembers how at the end of last term they sat in Penelope's room and drew up goals for the next semester. Alex was going to make dean's list despite Penelope's protest that "you've already done that, darling." Penelope was going to find a man: "a beautiful, straight, and experienced one."

Caroline lied and said hers was to find a new major, but it was really to find out how to like herself. She has this idea that if she likes herself more, she will need to like the other two less. If the need is less, the liking would be more. Maybe.

"It may be gross, Alex, but it works."

"Hmm," Alex says with studied indifference. "So does a tampon."

"Now, that's gross."

"Actually, it keeps everything from getting gross."

"Alex, a tampon is one of those necessities one simply doesn't speak of. Menstrual blood is messy."

"Doesn't the diaphragm get messy... you know, after?" Caroline asks.

"Don't know yet," Penelope says. "If I did, that would have been the most exciting part of my summer."

"Not if it was lousy," Alex says.

"Sex is only lousy, darling, if you let it be."

"Really?" says Caroline. "This is news to me."

Alex sends a wide and happy smile Caroline's way. "Me too," she says.

Someone knocks at the front door, and Caroline opens it. It is the UPS man with yet another package from Alex's mother. Penelope smiles at the man; Caroline watches Penelope do so, and Alex stares at the package in dismay.

"I don't believe it. Can I send it back?"

"Please, ma'am, just sign here."

"What is it?" Penelope asks.

"It's the goddamn mirror from the hallway at home. I told her a million trillion times that I did not want it."

"Why not? That dinky one in your bathroom will just let you look at your face."

"And that," Alex says, "is bad enough." She hands it to Caroline. "You deal with this."

Caroline unwraps a long rectangular mirror framed in heavy oak. She looks around the room trying to figure out which wall to put it on.

"It's going in the closet," Alex says.

"Why?" Penelope looks into it, checking her part. "I think it's pretty." She takes the mirror from Caroline and balances it on top of the bookshelf and against the wall. "There, see? Don't we look lovely," she says to Caroline. "Come here, Alex."

Slowly Alex approaches. When she was anorectic last semester, mirrors lied to her and she almost died. When she gained the weight back, mirrors told the truth and that makes her, occasionally, want to die. In the mirror she looks at Penelope's and Caroline's reflections first. Penelope seems sleek and polished, just like her new haircut. A little flat on top, but nothing else is out of proportion. She has hollowed cheeks and oval green eyes. She is not as pretty in repose as she is in movement because Penelope's beauty is in her "too muchness." She takes everything to extremes, and to watch her do so with a broom, a study book, or even a man is lovely. Caroline has perfect, heavy cheekbones and an almost Greek nose. Her face is broad and open, beautiful in the way a field or mountain is.

Alex looks at herself. She is wearing a baggy pink T-shirt to camouflage her bosom, which she thinks is too large and therefore fat. She brushes her gold-brown hair out of her eyes and sees a round face with a not-quite-pointy chin and a snub nose with a small bump on the bridge. Nothing to die for, but nothing that bad, either. She turns sideways and decides that if she is not as thin as *Vogue* advocates, she is not fat, either. She looks at her friends, who are also looking at her, each other, and themselves, and then back at herself.

She sees that, as a group, they are not pretty girls in the classical sense. They do not look like the women who stride down Fifth Avenue in black tights and short dresses leaving a trail of perfume and gaping men. She sees that despite major differences of hair and eye color, she and her friends look strangely alike, though not alike in the way of fashion models who populate every ad in the world.

She does not see that this will both save them and destroy them.

"Put it in the closet," she says firmly. "I simply can't believe that classes start tomorrow and I haven't even organized my desk."

"Classes." Caroline groans. "I got closed out of almost everything."

"Thank God you're in Russian," Penelope says happily. They are both Soviet studies majors, and Penelope knows she cannot go it alone in learning the language. The professor gives a quiz every day.

"Yes," Caroline says, "that's about all I got. Are you still in History eleven, Alex? I might try to pick it up."

"Yes." Alex turns to Penelope. "Do you like the English we have?"

"I like everything I have, darling," she says.

"Me too."

Alex and Penelope smile at each other, enjoying their mutual glee and satisfaction.

"Well," Caroline says, "I'll have to go on campus tomorrow and find a good elective. Any ideas?"

Alex frowns. "Come with me to comp. lit. Dr. Jordan is very good. He knows ten languages."

Penelope and Caroline laugh.

"Sanskrit, too," Alex says.

Everyone who converges on campus in late August for the second, third, or fourth time knows what to expect. On the first day of classes, the paper will put out forty pages of useless information. Girls with freshly curled hair and Baby Love perfume will go through sorority rush and cry when the best houses cut them. During home football games, you can have a whole floor of the library to yourself. The drama department will put on pretentiously intellectual productions of everything from *The Importance of Being Earnest* to *Three Penny Opera*. The rugby team will show *The Graduate* to raise money for new equipment. People will go and laugh at the plastics line, and seniors will pretend to laugh when Hoffman's father asks what four college years were worth. But they will go home and have nightmares.

Alex is not having a nightmare, but the steady metallic scratching noise at the front door wakes her up, very fast, very scared. Her clock says 2:40, and she catches her breath. It is just Cristen getting into the apartment. Now she is in the kitchen, now in the bathroom, finally in her own room, door shut. But still Alex can hear her. Closet opening, dresser drawers slamming, the sound of a radio as Cristen adjusts the alarm, and the bed giving way to a familiar weight.

Alex punches her pillow and tosses off her quilt. She is already tired of having her dreams disrupted by Cristen. She pushes a sweaty strand of hair off her face and curses silently. They don't make apartments in North Carolina the way they do in New York, she thinks.

"Does it occur to you that the fact that we pay three hundred a month and your parents pay thirteen hundred and not the state accounts for the wall's thickness?" Cristen would demand if she could hear Alex. Cristen is from Charlotte and likes to remind Alex not to be a snot about the fact that she is a New Yorker.

Alex was dreaming that she was Cathy in *Wuthering Heights,* and she knows that she will not be able to get back to Heathcliff's arms tonight. Penelope would say that Alex is taking her studies too, too far. Alex and Penelope are taking English 97—"Genesis of the Female Novelist"—together. They have just finished *Wuthering Heights.*

Penelope is frequently telling Alex what she is doing wrong ("Because I love you, darling"), so Alex decides, while rolling in damp sheets, to keep her dream private.

God, she would kill for an air conditioner. Maybe she can get her father to send her some money. He is very open to complaints about the South. He wanted Alex to go to Brown.

"Like half my senior class, Daddy?" Alex demanded. "I'll pass on that."

"You like them, Alexandria, I know you do."

"It's Alex, and I like a lot of people."

She does, but there was something about her classmates that made Alex feel she was failing as a teenager. She did not smoke, drink, do drugs, take the pill, or go to Area. In North Carolina people assumed she did, that she had spent her formative years snorting her allowance away. In Chapel Hill, where almost everyone grew up in a small and southern town, Alex could revel in a reputation she did not have to lift a pinkie to earn.

Only Penelope knows better, but it is okay, because Penelope left Paris for much the same reasons Alex rejected Brown. Edward knows better, too, which is not as okay as Penelope knowing. Edward had gone to the all-boys high school across the street from Alex's coed one. He had dated some of Alex's classmates, but never Alex. Once they got to Chapel Hill he told her she had a reputation, just not the kind any respectable woman of the eighties wants: "One of those smart, tight-ass ones that doesn't put out," was Edward's phrase. He could have just told her yesterday, so loud and clear is every word in Alex's memory. When he began to take Caroline out, Alex had a vague sense of discomfort, but nothing like now, now that they have broken up. Alex wonders if Caroline doesn't sometimes hold her guilty by association.

The red neon light of Alex's clock says that it's 3:10.

"Jesus." Alex pulls on the running shorts she laid out

beside the bed for her morning run. I'll just get a six-hour jump on it, she rationalizes. She is aware that she has been running a whole lot lately, but she doesn't think it's obsessive yet.

Last year, when she was a freshman, it had become obsessive. Last year she couldn't even talk to anyone if she hadn't gotten her five miles in. She laces her sneakers and makes as much noise as possible going out of the apartment. Fuck Cristen.

Alex lives in an apartment complex halfway between the firehouse and police station on Airport Road—at the bottom of a hill. This is always the hardest part of the run. She crosses North Street, then Rosemary, before she reaches level ground. She jogs in a tight circle while deciding on a course; she'll just pass Penelope's house on Carr Street and see if the light's on.

Penelope takes a last swallow of coffee and, putting down the empty mug, looks at the clock on the wall: 3:15, it says. Impossible. Her gold bracelet wristwatch says 2:20. One of the fuckers is wrong. She has the feeling it is probably after three. Shit. She throws her Russian grammar book at Caroline, who is sprawled out on the couch going through vocabulary flash cards. The book sails over Caroline's head and lands half a foot shy of the wall.

Caroline rolls over lazily and smiles at her friend. "Had enough?"

"Whatever, ever, possessed me to take Russian? I don't even like vodka, for God's sake."

"Knowing the language is a requirement for Soviet studies, Miss Samms, and there's not a fucking thing you can do."

"Don't call me that," Penelope says, pulling at her spiky blond hair. She is looking out the screen door thinking how nice and dark and warm it all looks outside.

"A large, lovely womb," she says.

"All right, Penelope, I say we call it a night." Caroline begins to sort her index cards. "You're babbling."

"No. I'm staying up till I know every rule in that book by your head. It just kills me that you're going to walk in there tomorrow and ace it. You're just staying up to humor me."

Caroline doesn't say anything.

"At least Alex is like me," Penelope says querulously.

"Alex studies. She studies a lot," Caroline says, snapping a rubber band at the U2 poster over the fireplace.

"Yes, darling, but she needs to, not like some people I know."

"Everyone needs to study, Penelope, but not the morning of the test."

"I'm not stupid. I understand most things. Why is the genitive plural beyond my grasp?"

"Because it's sheer memorization, and you're much better at analyzing and arguing and truly knowing something. Anyone can memorize."

"Lord, I love you, Caroline. You do know what to say."

"I know. I think with great clarity." Caroline bites out her words.

"What?"

"This summer I was helping a summer intern at my father's office with a brief. We were at his apartment and it was sort of dimly lit and we were alone and he looked up and stared into my eyes and said, 'I'm sure you've heard this before, but you think with such clarity.' It was classic. A normal woman would have been told how beautiful she was."

Penelope laughs. "It's a small price to pay for being smart."

"On the contrary, I think the price is enormous. There is no real substitute for being told you're beautiful."

"Except an A in Russian!"

"Hi, can I come in?" It is Alex, whose red T-shirt is sticking to her chest and whose long hair is pulled straight by sweat.

"Don't you look loverly," Caroline says, opening the door for her.

"Alexandria, darling, how is your Russian?"

"Nonexistent." Alex flops onto the couch.

"Careful, you're lying on six very important quizzes."

"Already six?" Alex asks, handing the sheaf of papers to Caroline.

"We have one every class period, darling. It's a Monday/Wednesday/Friday class. Go figure."

"Cristen woke me up again," Alex says in a loud and aggrieved voice.

"Do be quiet," Penelope says. "You'll wake the others." Penelope has two housemates, and neither of them has a quiz tomorrow.

"Well, good, I feel like doing unto others what has been done unto me."

"Alex," Penelope says in a soft deceptive voice, "if she's making you so crazy, why don't you just move out? I could fix up the little room for you."

Caroline heads for the kitchen, which is right off the living room. She has heard this conversation before. She takes a jam jar and fills it with water. Sitting at the kitchen table, she flips through an old issue of *Interview,* not really looking at anything. She, too, has a difficult roommate, but Penelope has never offered to "fix up the little room." She can hear Penelope reciting some of the stranger rules of grammar (the masculine noun in gen plural always ends in "ovo" except in the following twenty-seven exceptions) and Alex's happy laugh.

Last year, when she introduced them, it did not occur to her that her best friends would become better friends. But why not? Caroline thinks, tossing aside the magazine. She likes them for different reasons, and those reasons complement each other, the way best friends do. Alex was her roommate last year, and Penelope was the only other freshman in Russian for majors. She puts her glass in the empty sink and stares at it. It's tall and has an interesting pattern on the sides. It looks bad just sitting in the sink like that. She goes back into the living room.

"Look, guys, it's almost four. I'm going home. You going to run back, or you want a lift to your apartment, Alex?"

"Oh, Alex, stay. I'll show you the new skirts I got at The Limited."

Caroline knows the attraction this holds for Alex. The Limited is the only store in the Chapel Hill area Penelope will shop at, and when she does she always gets something Alex can acquire. Penelope shops with determination and fierce concentration, like a jaguar stalking prey. She never makes a bad selection and has picked out three of Alex's best outfits and two of Caroline's.

Alex looks briefly at Caroline, who is tossing her keys from hand to hand. Caroline looks back at her, not blinking, and keeps tossing the keys.

"Penelope, I'm far too out of shape to jog home. I'll meet you tomorrow."

"Your loss, darling."

"I know."

In the car Alex plays with the radio dial.

"Leave it," says Caroline. She is tired and bored.

"Everything okay, babes?"

"Yes."

"We never got to talk about your summer. It was okay, wasn't it?"

"Alex, I hate that word—'okay.'"

"Excuse me. Your summer was nice?" she asks, underscoring *nice* in a particularly nasty manner.

"It was lovely. Being in Colorado, clerking in my father's law office, looking forward to postcards from you in Greece, and from Penelope in Paris, and letters from Edward in New York, which never came."

"Penelope and I wrote you," Alex says. But for Caroline it just underscores Edward's silence.

"Yes, you did write me," Caroline says, pulling into Alex's driveway. "And it is always a joy to hear from you, Alexandria."

"Cool it on the 'andria,' would you?" Alex starts to get out of the car but pauses. "Caroline, would you like me and Penelope to stop being friends with Edward? Would it make things better with us?"

Caroline is aware that Alex's "us" means the three of them, and she does not have the words to explain that what would make it better is a return to two twosomes. Her very pores seem to ache when she hears of Penelope and Alex doing something with each other.

She remembers introducing them at a tea party Penelope gave in her small dorm room.

"Penelope, this is my roommate, Alex Rust. Alex, this is Penelope Samms." Caroline sashayed from the right to left foot. Penelope liked very few people, and Alex had already said, several times, "I am tired of hearing about this English chick, even if she is American. No one can be so wonderful."

"Hello, Alex, how very nice to meet you. I understand you're from New York. I must live there someday." Her tone implied that until she arrived in New York, it really couldn't be much. Alex shot a look at Caroline that said, Watch out. She shook Penelope's hand and said, "The pleasure, I'm sure, is all yours."

Caroline almost bit through her tongue, but miracle of miracles, Penelope laughed, and there was no separating them.

"Alex," Caroline says, closing her eyes, "everything is fine except that in five hours I have a major quiz on the genitive plural. Get some sleep, I love you."

Alex hears the car gun off and, watching the receding taillights, doubts Caroline's words. She sits on one of the cement steps leading up to her apartment. She can remember last year, when if she didn't see both Penelope and Caroline every day, she would become frantic. She would meet them for lunch, study breaks, anything. She loved them both so much that the enormity of it scared her. More than when the doctors had told her to start eating or they were going to put her in the hospital. The love is still there, but the fear has changed: now she is afraid that the love will lessen and that not seeing one of them for a day or two will be no big deal.

Alex shakes her head and walks up the steps. She cannot imagine time spent with either friend as no big deal.

Last year Alex had taken Caroline out to dinner at La Residence, the only French restaurant in Chapel Hill (and the most expensive), to celebrate their getting into Phi Eta Sigma—a freshman honors society.

"Alex, don't you think this is a bit much for getting good grades?" Caroline asked, studying the menu's exorbitant prices.

"Of course it's a bit much," Alex said, shaking her head. "But then the check my father sent me was a bit much, and I can't think of anyone I'd rather spend it on than you."

"Not even Chip Walters?" Caroline asked, referring to Alex's main squeeze of the moment.

"Caroline," Alex whispered in a tone conveying both great secrecy and disgust, "Chip is a boy."

They'd both giggled.

"Penelope says that your attitude towards men isn't mentally healthy," Caroline told her roommate while fighting with the cheese in her onion soup.

"Oh, Penelope," Alex scoffed. "She thinks anyone who doesn't screw through life is mentally unhealthy."

"Alex!"

"Well, it's true."

"No, it isn't."

"All right it isn't. Have it your own way."

After dinner they walked back to their dorm because Alex said she'd just gained ten pounds and Caroline could get her car from the restaurant in the morning.

They lived on South Campus, which was very far from everything, and Alex said how glad she would be for next year to come when she'd be out of dorms.

"Are you moving in with Penelope?" Caroline asked. She sounded wary.

"Penelope? No, of course not. There's no room at the house she's moving into, and she wouldn't be able to bear me. I wish you wouldn't be so stubborn about staying in the dorm and we could move out together."

"I'm not getting paid a huge scholarship for being here, Alex, and I haven't got a daddy liberal with checks."

"Right. Sorry."

"The funny thing is how Penelope is always hard up for cash."

"She spends too much." Alex shrugged and slipped off her pumps, which were cutting into her heels.

"Yeah, but her dad's got to be loaded."

"Oh. Why?"

"Well, he's an ambassador."

"I guess that doesn't make you rich."

"No, but you know who her family is, don't you?"

"I don't particularly care," Alex said, wondering idly how they always wound up discussing Penelope.

"She's a Samms."

"No shit."

"Her family's fortune comes from vacuum cleaner bags. One of her great-great-uncles invented them. They're absolutely rolling in money, the whole lot of them. After the war, her father took his inheritance and invested in a British publishing house. That's what he was doing before they sent him to Paris."

Vacuum cleaner bags. It sounded ridiculous to Alex. She thought of the busy way Penelope swept out her dorm room, how she chewed an apple thirty times before swallowing, how she read *Vogue,* asking everyone's opinion before turning the page.

"I love her, not her dad."

Caroline stopped. She grabbed Alex's hand. "Alex, do you love me?"

"Of course, silly."

"Good. I love you."

Caroline's words were sincere and just a little fervent. Alex was embarrassed. "I know."

In her mind and in letters home, Alex referred to her roommate as the space case, for the way Caroline behaved without her contacts, like a bat out of hell. In her underwear and bra, Caroline was a big pale glob, searching for her jeans, flannel shirt, and saline solution. She was the only person in the world who could make Alex laugh before her eight o'clock class. When Alex lost twenty pounds in just over a month, it was Caroline who called Dr. Rust and got Alex to a doctor who specialized in anorexia. When Caroline decided she was in love with Edward, not just in like, it was Alex who stayed up listening to Caroline list all the great things about the guy who was fast becoming Penelope and Alex's favorite "male friend"—a Penelope word for a male who is not sexually accessible, either because he is taken or prefers men.

Caroline never sneers "American" at something that displeases her. Tonight, as Alex steps into the shower, it occurs to her that gaining a friend at the expense of another is not worth it, even if the friend gained is Penelope.

She knows that Penelope is the star among the three of them. She drives too fast and smokes too much and doesn't like anybody. It's natural, therefore, that it become doubly important that she like them. When Penelope likes you, she takes you on picnics to University Lake, she buys ice cream and blueberries, she lets you raid her closet, she tells ridiculous and, Alex suspects, made-up stories about her family. She is wonderful; Alex loves her to pieces. When Penelope doesn't like you, though, watch out, you could be dead. Alex has seen it happen. It's amusing, but frightening. That is Penelope—fun and scary—like an adulterous love affair.

At five-thirty Penelope closes her book and stumbles up to bed. She should not be so wrought up over a simple grammar quiz, but she cannot send home another unsatisfactory report.

"One of the advantages, darling," she can hear her father say as he did repeatedly during this summer, "of your going back to America for school is that it wouldn't be as rigorous as a European university. A three point one for someone of your talents is just silly."

That she got a 3.1 without any studying at all would not be advisable to point out. Her father would want to know what she was doing instead, and as much as Penelope would like to say, "Fucking men and having abortions," she could not. Her father can always tell when she lies.

Slipping on her nightgown, Penelope remembers trying to explain to Caroline about her father.

"But, Penelope, you're over eighteen," Caroline argued. "The scholarship pays your tuition. Tell him to back off."

Tell her father to bugger off? No, she cannot even picture it. Alex understood immediately.

"He won't let go, and until you're ready, you won't make him. As long as you're home only three months, he can't do any major harm."

Yes, Penelope thinks, I am only home three months, but he's with *me* always.

"Let's exorcise him," Alex would say. She frequently pretends to be a satan worshiper. It's her defense mechanism against the Baptists who roam the campus, stopping you to ask if you have a reason to live. Oh, darling Alex, how do you exorcise blood? Even my "darling" is an exaggerated use of his deadly "darling."

"Darling, not another hairstyle?" he has said repeatedly.

Or, "Do you really have room for that, darling?" referring to Penelope's new plaster bust of Keith Richards, which took two months to make.

Or, "Oh, darling, not again," when Penelope came home, expelled, from yet another boarding school.

It is six o'clock before the deluge of her father's "darlings" sings her to sleep. Her Russian class is at nine.

"Edward, Edward, hold up a minute!" Alex calls down the long hall of Greenlaw, where they both have English classes.

Edward stops. "Hello, Alex, dear. How're things with my favorite Manhattanite?"

"Oh, shut up," she says, shifting her bookbag from her left to right hand. "I need your advice on something."

Edward laughs. "Alex, you only need advice when you have a date or a history exam. What is it this time? A volume of Marx or my vast experience as a man?"

She looks at him quickly and then lets her hair fall in her face. There is in Edward a basic elegance that no amount of rudeness or raggedy clothes can mask. His movements are careful without being deliberate, and his charm seems to lie in his very lack of it. Right now, Alex feels it her duty to point out this lack.

"Marx I can get in the library, and I haven't noticed

that you have a vast experience in anything except being a jerk."

She starts off, but he is quicker than his gangly height would suggest.

"Alexandria," he says, drawing out all the syllables in the name. "Why is it I can never escape without offending you?"

Alex leans against one of the grainy plaster walls. "I don't know," she says. "But you do a goddamn good job."

"I didn't have any problems offending you this summer," he says, smiling down at her, and it occurs to Alex that maybe she and Penelope like Edward so much for the simple reason that he is taller than they are.

"That's because you were writing," she says. "And it's harder to offend with pen and ink."

"All right, accept my contrite apology, dear, and tell me on what I can advise you."

"Well, it's about letters, really. I think Caroline is quite annoyed that you didn't write her over the summer, and I was wondering if it wouldn't be best that we just not let slip that you wrote to me."

"Alex, you are my friend. Caroline is an *ex*-girlfriend. I don't see any reason why I should lie about being in touch with you to a girl I hardly speak to anymore."

Is there such a big difference between girlfriends and friends? Alex wonders. She is smart enough not to ask this aloud.

"Really, Edward, it would make things easier for me. Is that so hard to understand?"

"No, Alex, I got it. Sorry to be so dense."

"It's okay. I know it's just programmed in your genes."

2

The Amazon Club

Penelope and Alexandria are sitting on the steps outside the cafeteria, drinking Tab and watching the students stream through the Pit to classes.

They are taking a study break.

They've been here an hour.

They are playing "scrutiny," which entails taking every vaguely interesting passerby and analyzing his or her hair, clothes, and overall look. It's harmless, it's fun, and they are sure other people do it to them all the time.

"That guy is sex personified," Penelope says, pointing to a passing figure.

Alex shrugs. "Penelope, he thinks he's Sam Shepard. Blue jeans and a flannel shirt in this weather?"

"It's the kind of shirt that you have for ten years, and it becomes so worn out all the flannel leaves. It's like wearing a T-shirt."

"I bow to your greater wisdom on the topic of clothes. Look, *he's* cute," Alex says.

"Too thin."

"I like them that way. I hope it will rub off on me or something."

"Alex, you are plenty thin, just crazy." Penelope spent so much time last year watching Alex eat or not eat and talking about food that she is particularly intolerant of letting Alex's weight phobia rear its ugly head again.

"Hmmm."

"There is too much light blue on this campus," Penelope declares.

"It's not light blue. It's Carolina blue."

"That doesn't mean everybody has to wear it."

"Penelope, remember that these are the same people whose cars have bumper stickers saying, 'If God is not a Tar Heel, why is the sky Carolina blue?'"

"My car doesn't say that."

"I know. Your car says 'Uppity Women of the World Unite.'"

Penelope laughs. "Well, it should."

In another hour Alex will have a sunburn, and Penelope will swear that she has gotten better tan lines. The Pit is paved entirely of red brick and can feel like an oven sometimes. Because it is smack in the center of campus and surrounded by the university's most important buildings —the cafeteria, student store, both libraries, and the Student Union—it is hard to remember, especially underneath the South's fierce yet lazy heat, that another world exists or could even intrude. There's far too much going on right in the Pit to make room for anything foreign.

In the afternoons starting around eleven, the Pit begins to fill up: a raving born-again preacher on one side ("Repent and God will be with you") and the Lacrosse Club sitting at a table on the other end, trying to drum up membership. Between the two sickly-looking trees that manage to live from year to year drawing nourishment from the small gray squares of dirt in the sea of brick hangs a big banner made of white sheets and acrylic paint and exhorting you to see Max Robinson give a lecture on journalistic ethics or to give blood in the Great Hall.

This afternoon it proclaims: "Only five days left to sign up for Sorority Rush—So RUSH."

"Christ," Alex says, looking from the white banner unmoving under the hot sun to the lunatic Baptist, moving only too much, "I don't know what's worse: being asked to join Jesus or a sorority."

Penelope, who has her eyes closed and can feel the sun seeping into her skin, slowly changing its color, laughs softly.

"I saw Robert for the first time today since my last story," Alex says. Robert is the arts editor at the *Daily Tar Heel.* "He does not compliment me wildly or say hi."

"Of course not. You said he has no social class."

"No, Penelope. I said he had no manners. Big difference there between class and manners."

"Right. One you're born with, one you can acquire, and only those born with it can tell the difference."

"Penelope Samms!"

"Darling?"

"Well, anyway. He's started a music column, and last

week he told me he wants me to write the next one."

"You?" Penelope laughs, thinking of Cher.

"Yeah, see it's not really about music, it's about politics."

"What are you writing on, U2?"

"No. Robert thinks it's interesting that whereas Helen Reddy's 'I Am Woman' used to be the song of the women's movement, he thinks Madonna's 'Material Girl' is more appropriate. It really pissed me off. Madonna's song, besides being yet another sexual come-on, is really about men. How to select them, what to do with them, et cetera. It negates all progress women have ever made and isn't really focused on them the way Helen Reddy's is."

Penelope always has trouble following Caroline's and Alex's "feminist" talks, and now she has an idea why.

"Who," she asks, "is Helen Reddy?"

"You've never heard of her? I'll lend you the record. My mom got it when she went back to medical school. All the other women had it. She thought it was required."

Penelope laughs. "I have a horrendous Bullfoot story to tell you."

"Wonderful," Alex says without interest.

The Bullfoot is the name of the scholarship responsible for Alex's and Penelope's trek to North Carolina. It was set up by a tobacco giant of the nineteenth century who was much taken with the ideals of the Rhodes scholarship and decided that such students could be bred at the University of North Carolina as well as Oxford. It is given to worthy high school graduates in North Carolina and certain prep schools in the Northeast and in Europe. The scholarship includes a built-in, undeserved prestige, especially for out-of-staters who tend to segregate themselves from the rest of campus. Professors take an added interest in them; other students are frequently intimidated and often label them as "out-of-state Bullfoot," which is to say, "I've seen your kind before and will see it again before I leave." Alex always feels that there are a hundred life-styles streaming past her that she is missing out on: dark, exotic bohemians and kelly-green debutantes. She misses them because she is a Bullfoot. Penelope tends to wield the scholarship like a sword, perhaps feeling that mixed with her hodgepodge background, the Bullfoot makes her invincible.

Despite the fact that she is grateful to the Bullfoot foundation for giving her a lot of money for having done well in high school, Alex has little interest in Penelope's frequent stories.

"You know that South Africa seminar I'm taking? Where the professor's such a rotter?" Penelope asks.

"Yes, the one who fought in Vietnam and says no other human experience can compete with that?"

"Bingo. Can you imagine what Caroline would think of him?"

"I think she'd like him." Caroline's brother died in Vietnam when she was seven. Caroline cried when she told Alex that. Alex wonders if such a loss can compete with the human experience of actually being in Vietnam.

"Well, this morning he gave some poor girl a real walk-over, humiliated her in every way," Penelope says.

"And it was a stuck-up Bullfoot, right? Great!" The Bullfeet, especially out-of-state ones, are notorious for their ridiculous egos.

"No, it was just some kid from Greenville. Afterwards Kate stops and asks her if she'll keep the class."

"Kate Poser?" Kate Poser was in Alex's English class and had confessed to wanting to be just like Renata Adler. Renata Adler and *The New Yorker* are Alex's least favorite things about living in Manhattan, so anything Kate did really cracked Alex up.

"Yes. So the girl goes, 'Sure I'll keep it. Why not?' And Kate says, 'Well, most of us in there are Bullfoots with topnotch high school educations; you might not be able to hack it.'"

"Oh, Christ. What did the girl say?"

"'Bully for you, Bullfoot,' and then walked away, leaving Kate with a mouth hanging down to her nonexistent chest."

They laugh, and then Penelope says, "Listen, I'm changing my major."

"From Soviet studies? How come?"

"I failed the genitive plural quiz. I figure if I can't master twenty-seven exceptions to a complicated rule, I better give up while it's still easy."

"So are you going to drop the course?"

"Obviously."

"Why don't you try and take comp. lit. with Caroline and me?"

"No way. Caroline says that reading list is a mile long. She's going to drop."

"It *is* a lot of reading, but it's the kind of stuff you're supposed to read. Dante, *Don Quixote, Faust.*"

"Dante? Boring," Penelope says in an even, dead voice.

"Yeah, but Dr. Jordan really makes them interesting."

"Oh, Alex. Not again. It's the professor you like, not the books."

"It is the books I love. I just keep thinking it's an undying passion for the man teaching it."

The girls laugh, and suddenly Penelope gives Alexandria a nudge.

"Look, Alex," she says. "That's Edward's new girl, Susan."

Alex watches the waif Penelope has pointed out. She is dressed in white and carrying a Coke. Normally Alex hates it when a girl is identified through a boy, but in this case it's deserved. Susan will never be anything else but "somebody's girl." Alex says as much to her friend.

"But she's pretty," Penelope tells her.

"So?"

"Edward likes pretty girls."

"What about Caroline?" Alex asks.

Penelope pauses. That Caroline nearly clears six feet, has very short hair, and, when viewed from the back, is often mistaken for a boy, rarely occurs to her. Caroline is not a Bullfoot and takes every opportunity she can to tell people like Kate Poser how full of shit they are. She's the only person Penelope and Alexandria know who reads the *New York Times* from cover to cover. And *Foreign Affairs.* Both girls love her, but Penelope supposes, when she thinks about it, that she would never make the cover of *Vogue.*

"I'd forgot, you know," Penelope says. "I never think of her through him. With Caroline he really liked her as a person, and it was sad 'cause I knew it wasn't the way for him that it was for her. She wasn't a pretty girl, you see, but he really liked her."

"You mean he liked her until a pretty girl came along?"

"Yeah," Penelope says.

Alex watches Susan's stiletto form disappear. "Life sucks," she says.

"Yeah."

♦ ♦ ♦

Susan sucks the last of the brown sugary liquid from the green-glass bottle and then aims the bottle at the garbage can. She knows she will rot her teeth, but it will also enable her to lose ten pounds in a week, if she does nothing but drink Coke. It's not that she thinks she's fat, exactly, but Susan always drops ten pounds when she gets a new boyfriend; it is sort of like a present. Some of them notice, some don't; she wonders if Edward will. She hopes so. She likes him (or that he's from New York, she hasn't decided which) a lot.

Turning from the garbage can, Susan surveys the Pit. Sitting on the steps are two of Edward's best friends, Penelope and Alexandria. Even their names are intimidating. She has heard Edward call Alexandria "Alex" but knows she would never have the nerve. Although they have all been introduced to each other several times, neither Penelope nor Alexandria can seem ever to remember her name. The last time Penelope said to Susan, "No, I don't believe we've met," Susan wanted to scream, "We've met, we've met three times! Is 'Susan' so hard to remember?" But just then Alexandria had broken in, saying, "Hi, Susan, how's the year treating you?" and then maneuvered Penelope away before Susan had a chance to answer. She'd heard all the excuses of course; Edward was anxious that she like his friends, and everyone she meets with him has a Penelope/Alexandria story, which excuses their so-called manners.

"Look, dear," said Edward. "Penelope's from Paris and London. Her father's an ambassador. You can't take her personally. She reacts against his tact. And Alex is from New York." Alex is from New York, Susan thinks, looking at the girl's wacked-out earrings. Well, I'm from North Carolina, like most people here, and we get taught to remember names. Her sour expression turns to one of horror; she's just seen Caroline cross the Pit. Susan ducks behind one of the picnic tables. Old girlfriends intimidate her.

Alex jumps up from Penelope's side; it is the first movement either of them has made in an hour.

"Caroline," she hollers, waving a Tab in one hand and with the other holding down the hem of the micromini Penelope has lent her.

Caroline catches sight of her two friends and calls, "Back in a sec," before going into the Pit Stop, a small snack bar adjoining the student store.

"Just what she needs," snorts Penelope. "Lunch. Look at that arse."

"We call it ass here in the States," Alex says dryly. "And anyway, it's no bigger than usual."

"And that, darling, is bad enough," says Penelope in her best drawing-room voice. It always makes Alex laugh, which, Penelope maintains, is reason enough to use it; if she offended some with it, well, fuck 'em.

Caroline comes out of the Pit Stop balancing a cup of apple juice, a sack of popcorn, and a container of vanilla yogurt.

"Hi, guys," she greets them, passing the popcorn to Alex and the yogurt to Penelope. "Bet you've been studying so hard you forgot all about lunch, right?"

"Right," Alex says, deadpan.

"You forgot a spoon," Penelope informs Caroline.

"Wrong again, Miss Samms. Here you are." Caroline

produces a white plastic spoon from her back pocket.

"This your lunch?" Alexandria asks Caroline, sipping her friend's apple juice.

"Yup."

"You on a diet?" Penelope questions, scraping around the container of her yogurt.

"Yup."

"Whatever for?" Alex asks, her voice full of disbelief. She does not believe in dieting; she believes in vomiting. She's been told countless times she is ruining her health, but none of her lecturers could find an alternative to her desire to "have my cake and eat it, too." It is not, Alex realizes, the most pleasant way to live, but it works.

Caroline looks first at Alex and then at Penelope, before facing front and answering.

"Have you seen the girl Edward ditched me for? Compared to her I look like a cow."

"He did not ditch you," Alex says in much the same tone she'd use when trying to impress upon a three-year-old not to cross the street against the light.

"Okay, he did not ditch me. However, she did, shall we say, follow fast upon my heels. Will you accept that?"

Neither girl can answer. It is too embarrassing.

"You will never believe what happened to me this morning," Caroline finally says.

"What?" Alex asks, sucking on a piece of ice she picked from Caroline's apple juice.

"You know that course Edward took last year that he said was so good?"

Edward, Penelope thinks, always Edward.

"Yeah, the philosophy one that talks about the value of a liberal arts education?"

"Right. I heard that there was still room in it, so I went

to see the professor to see if I can get in, and he says, 'Sorry, I'm saving the open places for men. I already have too many girls, and men talk more.' "

Alex spits her ice out. "No way."

"It gets better. 'Look,' I say, 'I'm very talkative.' He tells me I look talkative, but that he's still saving the places for men."

"How does one 'look talkative'?" asks Penelope.

"I don't know, but Edward used to say that I did look that way. I figure his new girl, being about half my size, is not talkative. So, I'm on a diet. If I have to be talkative, I don't have to look it."

"You can sue that professor," Alex says. "I'm sure he violated something."

"Not according to the Constitution he didn't. Now if I had been black, well, that'd be another story."

Penelope examines her nails.

"I'm sure there's something you can sue him under," Alex says.

"Oh, Alex, I don't care that much. Now if I could sue Edward, that'd be something. I don't know what for, but . . ."

"Bad manners?" Alex supplies, looking at Penelope.

God damn Edward, Penelope is thinking. He truly is behaving in an appalling way. She should really be going back to the library. She has this feeling Alex is a hundred pages ahead of her in their English class.

Fate works in mysterious ways, Alex thinks. But for the grace of God, I could be in Caroline's shoes. Last term she and Edward had had a little fling, before he started taking Caroline out. Even now Alex thinks "little fling" is too big a word for it. She'd certainly been crazy about him; he was very handsome in a tall, endearing sort of way.

Edward smells like old sweaters, the kind that have been to Maine and Cape Cod and seen the insides of an attic trunk once or twice. He has a way of really, truly listening and then putting your hysteria or anxiety into its proper context so that it becomes an ordinary worry. And yet he escapes being dull or overly rational.

That he'd been the "big catch" among the girls in her high school senior class added to his appeal. Also, Mrs. Wexell was a great friend of Alex's mother, and Alex and Edward had played together as babies when their mothers would meet for coffee. The idea of being involved with someone you'd met when wearing diapers seemed too clichéd to be resisted. Alex was sure she couldn't match him intellectually, especially after hearing him tell their History 106 teacher that he'd read Marx's *Kapital* and therefore would have to disagree with the interpretation of the *Manifesto* presented to the class. Now, Alex had read the *Manifesto,* but she wasn't sure she could present her own interpretation, let alone disagree with anyone else's. On the plus side, she was in the middle of one of her heavy anorectic stages—running and swimming miles every day, eating nil, and therefore very, very thin.

So she felt sure that even if he thought she was an idiot, he couldn't possibly think she was ugly. They'd gone out a couple of times, and when he walked her to her dorm room after a party, the most natural (nerve-racking) thing to do was ask him in. While waiting for her proffered cup of coffee to heat up, he took her hand and very cautiously kissed her (as if I might bite, Alex thought later). They kissed till the water boiled, and then she unplugged the pot and let him lead her to the bed. His hand found her breast and then lay there; she wondered if maybe childhood hang-ups were keeping him back. They kissed some more.

"What are you most proud of?" he asked.

This was unexpected; most guys at this stage asked if you were okay. Alex thought a minute.

"Of me," she answered, thinking of Diana Ross's reply to the same question when Barbara Walters asked it on one of her specials.

"Oh," he said, and they both stared at the cinder-block walls that made the room look like a cell. Alex thought about how stupid she'd probably sounded, but not for very long: they fell asleep.

He left at five A.M. after her polite but firm refusal to make love with him. That was when he let her know of her high school reputation.

"But it's okay, I guess we were wrong about some of it, though not all. I'd stay," he added by way of explanation, straightening his hair, "but I hate sleeping in my clothes."

Alex had gone back to bed feeling very pretty and very pleased.

Neither feeling lasted very long. Although they went out a few more times, he never again made any attempt to touch her.

He thinks I'm dumb, Alex would think when running.

He thinks I'm ugly, she would think when eating.

It was around this time that she taught herself to throw up. If she was dumb, that was not controllable; ugliness was. It didn't take a genius to see that in this day and age, weight—any weight above Twiggy weight—was ugly. Kim Novak had long since fallen by the wayside.

It never occurred to Alex that her refusal to sleep with him might be taken as rejection. It never occurred to her with any of them, which is how she thought of men: as "them."

"Well, darlings, with any luck, all our male problems will be solved by my party this weekend," Penelope says.

"Oh, Penelope." Caroline laughs. "Male problems never end. Unless you're dead."

"Glad to see the optimistic spirit is alive and well in the Amazon Club," Alex says.

"Amazon Club" was a name Penelope coined after observing a very drunk Alex tell a drunker quarterback that no, he could not feel her up because at birth one of her breasts had been chopped off to make it easier to shoot arrows for the sole purpose of castration. The quarterback had turned very pale, and Penelope, laughing in disbelief, had decided that no female under five feet ten could have the balls to say such a thing; thus the Amazon Club.

"Anyway, Caroline," Alex continues, "I maintain you are wrong. For example—I have a date tomorrow. I have been eating peanut-butter cookies all week, but I still have a date."

"You're coming to my party, aren't you?" Penelope asks anxiously. "I can't face it if you don't."

Despite several previous successes, Penelope is always convinced her parties will bomb, that no one will show up.

"Yes, of course I'm coming," Alex says. "I'll just bring him along."

"And just who is he? This lover of peanut-butter cookies?" Caroline wants to know.

"James Harrington."

"James Harrington," Penelope repeats. "He doesn't count."

"And why not?"

"You reviewed his play, you wrote an article about how great he is."

"Right, and to thank me for being such a discerning reporter, he wants to take me out."

"Apparently," Caroline pipes up, "he thinks he's just as wonderful as your article maintained he was."

"I know, it's great. I never have to think of anything to say. He does all the talking."

The Amazon Club dissolves into laughter and then disbands, promising to see Penelope Saturday night at her house.

"Be there or be square, as they say down heah," Penelope calls in her mock southern accent.

"Aloha," says Caroline, another southern favorite that cracks them up.

"Aloha," echoes Alex, holding down her skirt and running to the library.

That night the possession comes on Alex. It's a relief that she has a whole free evening, so she can do it without worrying about not finishing on time. She gets on her bike and flies down Airport Road to the nearby A&P. Cookies and Sara Lee cheesecake and of course some Life cereal. Ice cream? No, better just get a gallon of milk. She'll need the pure stuff to get all this crap back up. Once safely home, door locked, apartment mate out, she starts to eat. It's all she wants to do. She doesn't want to think about tomorrow and the problem of what to wear and why Edward dates Susan now and not her and her five finals in December: just eat, eat, and it all goes away.

When she's exhausted her groceries she goes into the kitchen and drinks a glass and a half of milk. In her bathroom she runs cold water over her middle and index fingers and sticks them down her throat. When it's all come up she drinks some more milk and tries again, just to be sure. The dry heaves follow, and she's clean; pure and empty. Her head hurts, her throat's sore, and she lies on her bed thinking, Never again, but that's bullshit. Complete emptiness and purity can only follow total violation and fullness. That's life, that's Alex's life.

"And one of these days," Alex can hear her mother say, "you're going to die from it."

"I know, Mom," Alex says aloud, from her bed, "but I'm going to die thin."

If Edward or anyone else were to ask Alex now what she is most proud of, she would not be able to say, "Me." Not anymore. A mature together person does not stuff herself to deal with her problems. A truly beautiful person does not have to vomit to get that way.

But if anyone ever again asks, "What are you most proud of?" she will have an answer. Playing with her earrings, Alex thinks about Susan. There isn't much chance that Edward would ever dump a girl who looks like that, and James Harrington will never stop talking long enough to catch his breath, let alone ask her that question. Still, Alex likes to be prepared.

Mr. Rust belongs to a club on Gramercy Park that every Christmas deigns to let women into its hallowed halls. Last Christmas Alex wore a shiny red dress with gold trim and five mismatched gold earrings. Wearing her mother's black pumps (dating back from the fifties), Alex stood close to six feet.

"You look like a dream, honey," her mother said, and for once Alex believed her and didn't cringe when her father introduced her as "my daughter, Alexandria." That night "Alexandria" fit.

The dining hall was filled with big round tables, and the Rust family sat with three men in white tie—total strangers. Two were typical club members, florid and white-haired—but the third Alex could not keep her eyes off of. He had chiseled features and close-cropped blond hair. He spoke and moved with ease and charm, and though he was entirely wrapped up with his business chums and never glanced her way, he was a pleasure to look at. When he got up to go to the bar, Alex followed him and stood by him, listening to him order a drink. He even smelled good.

I wonder if he knows just how great he looks, Alex thought. It would be nice for him to hear, and he's certainly made my evening. When her father brought the coats it occurred to her that men told women all the time how beautiful they were, and that was acceptable. She waved her father aside and leaned across the table.

"Excuse me, sir?"

He looked up. "Yes?"

"I just wanted to tell you that I think you're marvelous looking and a real joy to watch. You've made my evening a pleasure." With that she got up and walked away from the table, leaving, her mother said, three flabbergasted men, but one with a very pleased expression on his face.

"Alexandria, really," her father said in the taxi home.

"Really what? It's what I believed, and I would have been sorry not to have told him. You wouldn't have wanted me to be sorry about anything, would you?"

Mr. Rust slumped back in his seat. "No, dear, I just want you to be happy."

"Well, I am," she said. "Extremely."

The phone rings. Alex hopes it is not her mother, who can always tell when she has just vomited. Dr. Rust says her daughter's voice drops after a bulimic attack.

It is Celia. Celia Douglass and Alex went to school together, filled out college applications, cheated on midterms, and taught each other how to write a "really good paper" without reading the book. Celia goes to Jonesfeld, an exclusive all-girls school in Jonesfeld, Massachusetts, and last summer went to Greece with Alex.

"Hi," Celia says. "What are you doing home on a Friday night?"

Alex almost says, "Vomiting," but remembers she managed to keep this practice a secret from Celia all summer. No mean trick when sharing a bathroom. "Studying," she says.

"Oh, my God, classes just started this week and I'm already behind."

"Celia, you make me sick. I've been in classes for three weeks."

"They start earlier in the South. You know that."

"What are you taking?"

"Mostly art history. You would not believe how hard it is getting."

"Celia, you could pass art history with your eyes closed. You've spent your entire life training to run an art gallery."

"I know, it just seems that everything is getting harder. By the time I've gotten out of bed, showered, dressed, I'm exhausted."

"Have you tried coffee?" Alex sits up on her bed. When she lived with Caroline last year, she would watch the magic coffee performed every morning.

"It's not that simple."

"Hey, are you okay?"

"Yeah. I'm probably just not eating right."

"Why? I know a little bit about this sort of thing."

"I know," Celia says. "It's not anorexia. Believe me. Things just seem to have lost their taste."

"Can I do anything?"

"No, I just called to say hi. Maybe you could come up for fall break?"

Caroline and Penelope had mentioned going to the mountains. "Maybe. I don't know yet."

"I'll call you," Celia says.

"Take care. Thanks for calling."

"Yeah. Bye."

Alex replaces the receiver slowly. She had not asked Celia why she, too, was in on a Friday evening. Studying? Didn't sound like it. Could Celia have a vice the way she herself does?

Alex dials the Jonesfeld number.

"Hey, do you remember my red dress?"

"With the gold?"

"Yes," Alex says with delight. A friend who remembers these types of details is more valuable than anything else she knows of.

"Of course. You wore that to your father's club last Christmas."

"Right."

"You looked great. You always look great. It's just you can't really see yourself correctly."

"Are you sure?"

"Yes. You are talking to an art expert," Celia says. "I know a thing of beauty when I see it."

"So, you're okay?"

"Alex, I love you. I'm fine. Talk to you soon."

Alex tugs at one of her earrings and thinks about the gold ones she wore that night. Celia was right, she did look great then, and right now that party last Christmas is what she is most proud of still.

Feeling nice and empty, Alex speaks to the still air in her room. "That, Edward, is what I'd tell you tonight if you were in my bed."

3◇

Dancing with . . .

On the day of Penelope's party, Caroline goes shopping. She is reminded of a shirt her brother brought her, before shipping out, when she was seven. WHEN THE GOING GETS TOUGH THE TOUGH GO SHOPPING. She could hardly read at the time, but the shirt was in her favorite color, lilac.

"Really, Carl," their mother said. "What are you trying to teach her?"

"Nothing, Mom, but she does have a bad case of the gimme's."

"That's true," Mrs. Schrombs said.

Who doesn't have them at age seven? Caroline wonders, walking through the cool fake marble paths of the mall. She stops by the black directory next to a fountain where people are sitting, drinking from waxy paper cups. "You are here," a gold arrow proclaims, pointing to some spot on the map. Caroline sighs and leans against the glass-encased pillar. What should she get? Something really chi-chi, or super-casual? Fuck. Going to a party without a date is hard, especially if you haven't done it in four months. Going to a party with Edward was easy; she wore what was clean. After all, she wasn't looking for anyone, and not making an effort showed people that he didn't care what you looked like—he loved *you*.

Caroline lets out a short, hard laugh. She remembers Edward sitting on her bed.

"I love you, Caroline, I'll never be sorry for the time we spent together, but I don't want to go out anymore."

"You mean you don't want to go out to the movies and to dinner, or you don't want to go out with me in particular?"

"Caroline, you're making this more difficult than it has to be."

"Damn right. I'd like to make it impossible. See, Edward, I love you *and* want to spend time with you. Which puts us at sort of an impasse."

He rubbed his eyes. "Not really," he said slowly walking across her dorm room and getting his jacket. "Because, you see, I'm leaving. I'm not leaving *you*. I hope we'll always be friends. But I am leaving the relationship."

And he did. That had been last April, and it still hurt to

see him and not be able to embrace his tall, lanky body.

I don't understand myself, she thinks, moving aimlessly toward the stairway to the lower level. He wasn't the first she'd gone to bed with or loved, but he was the first to tell her she was beautiful.

Caroline's first lover had been a war buddy of Carl's—someone who came back. They'd been going out for two months, sleeping together, when he said one night over dinner, "You know, it's funny that Carl should have walked away with all the looks in the family, and then have them blown away in Nam."

Caroline had immediately left the table, never looking back, thinking, Bastard, bastard, you bastard.

"You have a look," Edward said. "You walk in the room and everyone knows it."

"It helps to be six feet." She laughed.

"Maybe," he said, "but I think it's mostly that you're beautiful."

And I believed him. For four months I walked around thinking not even Grace Kelly could touch me.

She passes the Garden Terrace and thinks about lunch, but she hasn't bought anything yet. She'll just use their bathroom.

"Can I help you?" asks a brunette in black pants and a white blouse.

"May I use the bathroom?"

"I'm sorry, but that facility is reserved only for patrons," the woman says in a frosty voice.

Facility? Caroline thinks. Give me a break. "Look," she says, "I'm two and a half months pregnant and forgot to take my protein supplement this morning. I'm going to keel over if I don't get to a bathroom."

"Right in the back to the left," the woman says hurriedly, pointing with her arm full of menus.

Caroline smiles. "Thank you." That one always worked like a charm. The first time she'd done it in front of Alex and Penelope they'd freaked. When she came out the two broke off conversation and spoke at once:

"How much money do you need for an abortion?" Alex asked.

"How are you going to take care of the baby?" Penelope demanded.

"What baby?" Alex asked. "She's not going to have it."

"She's pregnant, isn't she?" Penelope demanded.

She loves the way her two friends can talk to each other and make no sense at all. She knows she could listen to them forever.

Alex answers the phone all out of breath.

"Hey, baby, what's up?"

"Hi, Edward. I just got back from running. What do you want?"

"Pretty snappy, aren't you?"

"Look, I have a date tonight, and I only have four hours to decide what to wear."

"Bringing him to Penelope's?"

"Yes. Of course."

"Aren't you scared she might not approve?"

"She never approves. Do you want something?"

"Um, yeah. I want to know if I bring Susan, will it be okay."

"Well, I don't think Caroline will be terribly happy."

"I meant," Edward says, "will Penelope be nice or make me wish I'd never been born?"

"Never can tell with her, can you?"

"Shit. I had a terrible time at her last party."

"You did? I had fun."

"Yeah, of course. You danced with Caroline and Penelope, and none of you paid attention to anyone else."

"Well, no one was very eye-catching, maybe."

"No. It's just that you guys have very high standards."

"What's wrong with that?" Alex demands. "Oh. Scared you and Susan won't make the grade?"

"I'll see you tonight," he says tightly.

"This is the last party I'm ever giving," Penelope says, flopping down on the couch after having just maneuvered the stereo into the living room corner.

"Shut up, Penelope," her housemates say, going on with their chores.

Nancy is putting paper on the wall near the stairs so people can write on it. Belinda is making a lethal fruit punch.

"No one will come," Penelope says. She is thinking about her first fancy dress ball. She was only twelve, not really old enough to go, but one of her sisters finally relented and took her along.

"Now behave like a lady," her sister whispered.

And she had. She'd pulled at her strapless gown, eaten some crustless sandwiches, and watched the dancing from behind various pillars. The women weren't so interesting to look at. Of course she had five sisters, and after a while one woman dressed up looks like the next. But the men! They were moving fluidly, talking rapidly, eating and drinking, like black-and-white magicians. She loved the way they stood in clusters and how one of them might break away reluctantly and ask a girl to dance. The girls always said yes, and who wouldn't? Penelope would have committed murder to be danced around the floor, right under the chandeliers and the watchful gaze of the older women. But what she really wanted was to be part of that cluster, to watch the muscles in their faces as they chewed and smiled, to inhale the smell of starch and cologne and brandy. Watching her sister in the arms of a sharp-nosed blond, Penelope felt a pang. She wanted one of those for herself. It seemed to her that men might be things you could take home and keep as your very own, much better than a kitten. Which would she pick? Probably the brown-haired one in the corner who needed to throw his whole head and upper body back when he laughed. He was talking with some friends, occasionally sipping from his crystal glass and ignoring the young lady at his elbow. His health and exuberance gave his skin a smooth pink glow, and she thought he might just burst out of himself, he was so alive. I want that one, she thought fiercely just as her sister materialized to take her away.

"How do you go about getting men?" she asked on the ride home.

"Penelope!"

No one had an answer for her, but she decided that from then on, wherever she went she'd spend life in the center of attention, in front of the pillar instead of behind.

And she did stand at the center now, but that wasn't the answer to her question. Watching Caroline and Alex makes her wonder if there is an answer. Maybe she'll find one tonight.

"But what if no one comes?" she moans.

"They'll come," Nancy says. "Now go get dressed."

Pretty Girls

♦ ♦ ♦

Susan looks in the mirror. Her hair is hanging straight and smooth, just grazing her shoulders. Thank God the muggy weather has vanished; only yesterday she could tell her hair was beginning to frizz, which always makes her look like a poodle.

Susan turns to her bed, where her father's old tuxedo shirt is stretched out. She thinks she will wear it with a thin black belt and a new pair of patterned Christian Dior hose, or will that make her feel too hot? Her legs aren't dark enough to go bare against all that white. Shit. What will she wear? Edward will be here in twenty minutes, and she doesn't want him waiting in the sitting room of her sorority house too long. Any Bullfoot is a good catch, and while Susan loves her sorority sisters to death, she doesn't trust them farther than she can throw a squad car. Finally she settles on a pair of khaki shorts and a Hawaiian print top. She knows that Penelope will have something cutting to say no matter what she wears, so she might as well be comfortable. Nine-forty. She still has five minutes. Earrings. The diamond studs she got for graduation will have to do. Her father and stepmother gave them to her; her mother didn't give her anything. Susan hasn't seen her mother since she was thirteen, save for the occasional birthday visit. Mrs. Simmons ran off with another woman when Susan was in junior high. Susan doesn't like to think about this, and right now she wishes she knew where Alexandria bought her earrings; it's a constant source of wonder to her how many different pairs Edward's friend can wear at once. Alexandria has five holes, three in one ear and two in the other. Susan has heard Alexandria say that she is a compulsive earring shopper. It must be an expensive habit. She slicks some gloss on and looks down at her digital: 9:45. If she hurries, she can meet Edward on the porch so he won't even have to brave the doors of the sorority, which, if he's like Penelope and Alexandria, he thinks is a ridiculous institution. One last look in the mirror, and then she's out the door.

When they get to Penelope's, Susan is already fuming. Edward's greeting was not "You look good," or even "Hi," but "Won't you be cold in that shirt?" She has taken that to mean that he doesn't like it. Great. It doesn't help that the first person they see is Caroline, who takes Edward by the arm, saying, "I want to talk to you."

Susan looks around for Penelope. She knows she'll have to introduce herself again, but a familiar face would be nice. It's hard to tell what this room would normally look like; it's so full of people, clouds of smoke, and strange, loud music. There are people hanging over the stairway's bannister, reminding Susan ridiculously of the zoo. She sees Marianne Lucia, a Bullfoot from Connecticut who was in Susan's bowling class last year.

"Hi, Marianne." This very soft and nervous, but Marianne turns.

"Hi, Susan, having a good year?"

"Oh, yes. Are you?"

Marianne smiles. "Fair to middling. Don't you just love that girl's outfit?" She points to a figure in a black leather miniskirt and feather boa. "It's outrageous."

It looks hot and stupid, Susan thinks, but she rarely contradicts anyone. "Yeah, I like it."

"Oh, there's Malcolm. See you later, Sue." Marianne bounces off, and Susan is alone again. She presses up against the stairway railing, hugging her chest. She thinks if the music gets any louder, or the people any denser, she's going to disappear.

"Been ditched already, darling?" says a soft, lilting voice behind her.

Susan whirls around. "Penelope!"

"Yes?" Her eyes are amused and neatly outlined in a glittery green.

"Uh, hi."

"Hi," returns Penelope. "Enjoy yourself." A large tan hand suddenly appears on Penelope's breast.

Susan is pleased to see Penelope caught off guard.

"Colin, don't be a bother," says Penelope, taking the hand of one of the most beautiful men Susan has ever seen. He has the clear-cut features you see on the cover of *G.Q.* and softly feathered brown hair. His shirt is tight against his chest and stomach. He probably works out on Nautilus every day, Susan thinks.

"Susan, this is Colin Campbell. Colin, this is Susan something or other, Edward's new girl."

Susan feels as if Penelope had taken one of her neatly manicured hands and slapped her across the face. Penelope turns to go, Colin hanging on her arm, and then twists back to face Susan.

"Do me a favor, love," Penelope says. "If you see a girl wearing five earrings come in, tell her I'm in the kitchen."

"Sure," Susan says. "I know Alexandria."

"You do?"

"Yes, we have a class together. Of course it's really big, four hundred people, in Hamilton Hall—" Susan knows she is babbling, and Penelope cuts her off.

"How odd, how very odd that she didn't mention it yesterday." Penelope and the tan god depart again.

I knew it! Susan thinks. They were talking about me in the Pit. Great. Where the hell is Edward?

When Caroline sees Edward come in, Susan looking pouty right behind him, something in her head snaps. She thinks about the long breakfasts they would have had on Sunday mornings at Breadmans sharing the *Times*, arguing about the contras. Edward said they were too badly organized and splintered to tell what was really going on. Because Caroline had a brother who died in Vietnam when she was seven, she always left Edward exasperated and frustrated with the war cry of "No more Vietnams!" Caroline doubts if Susan even knows where Nicaragua is.

That's the void I've been feeling, Caroline thinks. I don't miss the sex. I miss the conversation. She puts down her drink. If only Alex were here, she could distract Susan. Caroline shakes her head. My God, I slept with him all of last semester. If he can't talk to me without her, fuck him. She approaches them, and without acknowledging Susan (in her best Penelope Samms manner), she takes Edward's arm and says, "I want to talk to you."

"All right."

They go outside and sit on Penelope's back porch. Inside, the Thompson Twins are pleading to dance across the sea.

"There's something that's been bugging me," Caroline starts off. "And you're really the only one who can help me out."

He doesn't say anything.

"You said we would still be friends, so I know you won't mind."

"What is it?"

"Now, I don't want you to get it wrong. I'm not jealous, just puzzled and disappointed. Why Susan? Was I so bad that you had to get my foil?"

"Caroline, I'm not sure this is any of your business."

"Dammit, it is my business! Do you know how this makes me feel? Was I an aberration, or is she? For God's sake, Edward, she wears add-a-beads!"

"No," he says slowly. "You were not an aberration. I don't know if I can answer 'Why Susan?'"

"You told Alex she had nice legs. Is that really enough?"

"My, Alexandria's becoming quite the little sieve."

"Alex has always had a mouth. You know that."

"Yes. Well, no, it's not Susan's legs."

"What, then?"

"I'm not sure I can give you an answer."

"Let me get this straight. You are taking out a girl whose I.Q. is no higher than two digits and you don't know why? That's good, Edward. Is her intelligence rubbing off on you?"

"Her I.Q. is not that low, and I don't think I took you out for your I.Q. level, Caroline."

"It helped."

"In the end it hurt. It's exhausting to be with someone who *always* has to be smarter. That's not a problem with Susan."

That's an understatement, Caroline thinks. "She has a sign on her forehead that says 'Space to let.' Haven't you seen it?" She knows this is a mistake, but it's too late.

He gets up. "Look, Caroline, I'm sorry you don't like the women I date. But I am not going to take out an Amazon just to please you." He leaves, and Caroline wonders if she has just been insulted and how Edward knows about Penelope's club. Probably Alex. Well, when she sees her tonight, she'll chew her out. Right now she's too tired to move.

Susan definitely has a headache. For a while she wasn't sure. The music is so loud that it took a while to figure out whether the pounding was inside or outside. It is inside.

"Hi, you look like you know as few people as I do."

Susan looks at the pleasant-faced girl on her right.

"My name is Terry Kapel." Terry has a slight southern accent. "I was Penelope's roommate last year. How do you know her?"

"I'm dating a friend of hers."

"Where is he?"

"Just don't ask."

Terry laughs. "It was nice of Penelope to invite me, but I forgot that we really do not have the same type of friends. Everyone here is wearing all black or six different colors that don't match."

"It's a definite scene," Susan agrees.

"A what?"

"A scene. You know how in the sixties and seventies there was always a scene? Like Warhol in New York. I always wanted to be a girl of the year."

"There are worse ambitions," Terry says. "But what would you do when your year was up?"

Edward reappears, saving Susan from answering this unanswerable question.

"Hi, Terry. Long time no see."

"Hi, Edward. It was nice meeting you, Susan." Terry heads toward the kitchen.

"What did Caroline want?" Susan asks.

"You heard her. To talk to me."

"What about?"

"For fuck's sake! What is it, tonight? The Spanish inquisition?"

"Sorry."

"Forget it. Let's dance."

With her head pounding the way it is, dance is the last thing Susan wants to do, but if it's what he wants, who is she to prevent him?

Penelope knows she is getting drunk, but that's okay. If she gets really plastered, she'll spend all of Sunday puking—good for a three-pound loss, at least. Penelope grimaces. If she doesn't watch it, she'll wind up like Alex, spending every waking moment stuffing her face or vomiting her guts into a toilet bowl. Well, I've got more on my mind than Alex's eating habits, Penelope thinks. As in where the hell is she, and why is Colin following me around? God knows he's smashing to look at, but it can't go anywhere, no matter how many times he puts his hand on my breasts. Penelope recalls Susan's look when Colin had done just that in front of her and laughs. What a twit, she thinks. Someone has replaced the Thompson Twins with U2, Penelope's favorite group, but right now she needs some air.

"Penelope, come and dance with me."

"Greg, let go of my arm." Greg Neals is a pale-skinned blond man with gray eyes that hold you better than a pair of arms ever could. He is the last person Penelope slept with. She remembers two things: that she has not had sex in four months, and that the person Greg slept with after her was a graduate student from Italy who looked like Sophia Loren.

"Come and dance, love."

She pats his cheek and smiles sweetly. He puts his arms around her waist. She thinks of Colin and says, "I can't think of anything I'd rather do less."

She watches Greg beat a hasty retreat and goes out onto her porch. There's someone leaning against one of the rickety posts.

"Caroline?"

Caroline jumps up. "Oh, it's just you," she says upon recognizing her friend. "Got a cigarette?"

"Yes." Penelope sees that Caroline has been crying: her eyelids are puffy, the way Alex's get on really bad vomitting days. She should probably inquire what's wrong, but tonight is her night, and she doesn't want to hear about Edward. She just hands her pack of Camel's over and watches the glow of the match.

"Caroline," she says suddenly, "what are the chances of Colin's changing his stripes?"

Caroline gives a short laugh. "Oh, Penelope, not again. Colin's as gay as they come. Can't you run after someone normal? A gay man after Greg Neals who sleeps with *everyone* on campus—*that* would be a mistake."

Penelope stiffens. "Greg happened to like me."

"Yes, yes, I know." Caroline's voice is tired. "But for how long? Three days, four, five?"

"A week," Penelope snaps, lighting her own cigarette.

"All right, a week. But Colin won't even give you a tumble. He's gay. You need a discriminating heterosexual."

Like Edward? Penelope wants to say, but she does not feel that mean. "How do you know he won't give me a tumble?" she asks instead.

"Oh, Penelope, give it up. His lover of the past three years just graduated last term. He's in acting school in Los Angeles waiting for Colin to join him this December."

"Well, for your information, he's been pawing me all evening."

"So, he's drunk."

"So, so am I. You never know. Ta-ta, darling." Penelope slinks out the screen door. She hesitates a minute. Caroline is lighting another cigarette. No. She will not ruin her own good time for heartbreak that should be over by now.

In the kitchen Colin grabs Penelope around the hips.

"There you are, my lovely goddess. I thought I'd lost you."

"Lose me? Never. I was just getting a drink. Follow me," Penelope says, leading him to the little pantry where she has stocked the booze.

"To the ends of the earth," Colin says, holding her hand.

That is the kind of line that would make Alex drop a guy quicker than a "hot potato," as they say in the States. But she loves it. Unlike the other members of the Amazon Club, Penelope finds looks and gallantry very important. Take Caroline and Edward. Now Penelope loves Edward; he's a dear, and he truly appreciates and admires her—but he's too skinny, and his hair always needs cutting. Alex says it's sexy. Ugh. She doesn't know how Caroline could have stuck with him or even now could cry over him the night of a party.

She hands Colin a bourbon and swigs hers down. Colin takes her empty glass and sets it down next to his. Hands on her breasts, he kisses her. His mouth is warm. She lets her hands travel. His hair is clean and soft. He smells like Aramis. She is in heaven.

"Penelope," he says against her neck, "it's different. It's very different."

She smiles. It is all she wanted to hear.

It occurs to Caroline that she does not have to sit here forever. She can go inside, find Alex, and leave. In the living room, Penelope's old roommate Terry and Greg Neals are talking. They must have met last term that one week Greg was with Penelope. Caroline smiles. Penelope was so happy. "He thinks I'm beautiful," she had said. "He takes me to dinner, not lunch, and he doesn't want my class notes. He wants *me.*"

Edward and Susan seem to have gone. No sign of Alex anywhere. Fine, she'll just go home now anyway. Everyone else is. Maybe she'll wake Deena Jane up and talk to her all night about men who like girls with a two-digit I.Q. That would be an interesting conversation, as Caroline suspects Susan and Deena Jane are interchangeable. Now if she can just remember where she parked her car.

When everyone has gone, Colin and Penelope stumble drunkenly up to her room. She lies on the large double futon watching Colin strip. He does it with great ease and dexterity; he clearly has a lot of practice taking his clothes off. He is so gorgeous. She likes the way all the muscles in his back move, as if they have direction and purpose in life. His arms are almost sculpted. Her own arms are functional and slender, but relatively shapeless.

The air conditioner is humming (to ward off the September southern heat), and so are her ears.

"You're so soft," he murmurs, slipping a hand under her shirt, unhooking her bra. "I want to look at you."

Part of Penelope is embarrassed. Undressing in front of a lover is so very hard. It doesn't help that a little voice in her head is screaming, Of course I'm soft. It sort of comes with the territory, you idiot! What the hell did you expect?

"You're the first one," he tells her, his hands everywhere.

First what? she wonders.

"Oh, I've betrayed Conrad with other men," he continues. "But never with a woman. A woman is so serious, somehow."

Penelope stops breathing so as not to laugh. It's like Alex says. Only a gay man will not use you for casual sex. A hetero, most definitely: he's programmed to; but never a gay.

"You're so lovely," Colin is saying.

"Colin, you're right. Sleeping with a woman is serious, especially for you. We're both a little drunk." Big understatement, she thinks. "And I don't want us to do anything that will make getting up any more painful than our hangovers will."

"You're like a goddess. But you're right, we'll go slow, one day at a time, because I want you. I really want you, Penelope." His breathing becomes heavy and regular.

Well, that's something he shares with straights, Penelope thinks, lying on crossed arms, looking at his profile. They all conk out, leaving you to stay awake, pondering what exactly they meant. Does he want a relationship with me? Is it me, or could it be any other woman? Or for that matter did he just want to cheat on Conrad? She remembers Conrad now: a pale, almost anemic-looking blond, who charged across campus on an old ten-speed bike. She wants to shake Colin awake, ask him if he loves Conrad, ask him what he meant by "one day at a time." Why don't men realize that talking is the best part of sex? She'll have to puzzle this all out tomorrow with Alex, after she gives her hell for not showing.

The air conditioner and Colin's breathing are steady and comforting, and, trying to distinguish between the two, Penelope falls asleep.

4.

Alexandria's Date: A Case Study

Alexandria studies James Harrington across the table in a booth at Swenson's. He is telling her about the reviews he got for a local production of *Exodus* in Wellfleet, where his parents have a summer house. The only thing she is enjoying in this monologue is his slight Boston accent; the way his "A's" come out with "H's" on the end and how some of his syllables are clipped, like Penelope's.

They have just seen the new Woody Allen film. Alex would like to ask him if he thought it was creepy the way Mia Farrow looked like an exaggerated version of Diane

Keaton. He does not, however, show any sign of running out of wind.

She toys with her butterscotch sundae. She is not sure if they will wind up fooling around, and she doesn't want to feel fat if they do. They held hands during the movie, but this guy may be happy talking all night. She doesn't even need to be here, and as a matter of fact she is behind in her English class, not to mention comparative literature. Does she have a quiz in history on Wednesday? Better call Caroline. If there was only some way she could sneak back to her apartment without his noticing.

He suddenly fires a question at her, making her drop the spoon.

"So what's Alex short for, anyway? Alexandra, Alexis, what?"

She cannot believe this. The byline of her article extolling his virtues was Alexandria Rust. "Alexandria," she says shortly.

"Alexandria?" he repeats, a blank look on his face. Maybe he is trying to think of how to parlay this into another monologue.

"Yeah. My mother was a Durrell fan."

"Come again?"

"Durrell. Lawrence Durrell, he's a famous writer. He wrote the *Alexandria Quartet.*" Beat. "That's four books."

"Oh." He leans over and takes one of her earrings in his hand. "So," he asks, "how come you have five holes?"

She removes his hand and smiles sweetly. "Actually, I have six."

It is the kind of thing you can say to a northeasterner. A southerner would pass out.

He leans back and looks at her. She feels a little like a

fly in a web. She runs her hand over the slippery vinyl of her seat to remind herself where she is. He signals for the check.

When they get to Alex's apartment, she is relieved to find that Cristen is out, at her boyfriend's house, as usual. Last year, when Alex was a freshman, Cristen took the new girl "under her wing." Alex would call her mother up and say, "I don't understand it. Cristen's a junior. Why is she spending all this time with me?"

"Maybe she likes you, Alex," Dr. Rust would say patiently, never failing to be amazed at her daughter's lack of self-confidence.

It wasn't until she had agreed to live with Cristen the next year that Alex realized why Cristen spent so much time with her—she had no other friends. She has a boyfriend, and that's it. No one in her dorm liked her, nor for that matter did anyone Alex introduced her to. People were polite, but they stayed away. Alex couldn't understand it, but now she's beginning to. Cristen doesn't just borrow Alex's clothes and earrings; she borrows Alex's "look," friends, favorite floor on the library—in short, her life. There is nothing independent about Cristen. Sometimes Alex feels as if she is living with *The Invasion of the Body Snatchers,* and while it's true she isn't having the best of times with James, she'd just as soon not have him distracted.

"You want something to drink?" she asks James, tossing her keys on the couch, where they land on three weeks' worth of *Daily Tar Heel*s. Alex saves them. She is thinking of making a scrapbook.

"Um, sure," he says, settling on the butterfly chair that used to be in the Rusts' beach house before they sold it.

Alex opens the refrigerator. There's half a bottle of Perrier and three apples.

Good going, Alexandria. You don't keep anything in the house. That way you won't eat, remember?

She pours the remainder of the Perrier into a coffee cup and brings it out to James.

"Great place you got here," he says, looking at the stark walls and decided lack of furniture.

"Well, we're both very busy, and decorating's pretty low on my list of priorities."

"Oh."

Just when we need it, he shuts up like a clam, she thinks. Typical.

"Would you like to listen to something?" she asks, bending over her stereo. "I've got Bowie, Springsteen, Steve Miller, um..." She trails off.

He has put his hand on her back, his tongue in her ear. Why do men think that's a turn-on? she wonders. It always makes me wonder when was the last time I used a Q-tip.

Suddenly he walks away. She watches him throw the yellow papers off the couch, sit down, and say, "Come here."

She does. This is her first date this semester, and she's not sure she's ready to throw him out. They kiss awhile, and she's surprised: he's very good. They're like the butterfly kisses she and her sister gave each other in summers at the beach: very slight, soft, gentle. He's also something of an acrobat. On a relatively narrow couch, he's managed to roll over on top of her without falling off. His weight feels nice, sort of safe, but Alex freezes as she hears him unzip his fly. She sits up abruptly, hand on the elbow of his unzipping arm.

"Um, I don't think so," she says softly.

"Why not?" He is already standing, tucking in his shirt.

She glances up at his face, decides that what she's reading on it is not good, and snaps out: "I don't want to." Oh, smooth, Alexandria, real smooth.

At the door he kisses her nose and says, "I'll call you."

Alex knows he won't and would rather he hadn't pretended.

After locking the door, she gets an apple and sits next to the stereo. Even Bowie's "Golden Years" cannot keep her "I don't want to" from reverberating through her head. It had sounded so hard and ugly just now with James. Not how she'd wanted to sound—this time. Three summers ago, yes, but not this time.

Three summers ago at the beach house, Alexandria said, "I don't want to, I just don't want to," over and over again, reminding herself of all the "Hail Marys" she'd never said but heard of from her convent-bred mother.

He had gotten her on the floor, and Alexandria would always regret that it hadn't taken more of a struggle. Two cracked ribs, a black eye, and a bloody nose was what she'd wanted. The memory of terror and the sick, sweaty, sour smell of his body wasn't enough. "I don't want to, I just don't want to." He uttered nothing, not even a verbal threat. "As if I were despicable, as though he couldn't bring himself to talk to me," Alexandria would explain later. "I don't want to, I just don't want to." When he was done, he stroked one of Alexandria's cheeks, and she broke her monotone chant and asked, "Why?"

"Every cunt needs a fuck," he said softly, and kissed her on the mouth, stood, and left her on the floor. On the floor of the kitchen in the family beach house that her father put on the market afterward and made a killing on. Alex knows that her father still misses the house, with its front deck, its yellow shaggy rugs, and the books that smelled of salt. Her father would sit on the deck before dinner and watch the sun bleed into the sea. Alex would sit on the deck after dinner and watch for the silver glints the sea would throw out at her as the tide came in. That's what she was doing that night. Her parents and sister were at the movies, and Alex pictured the evening stretching out before her, filled with solitude and beauty. She left the sliding-glass door open between the deck and living room so she could listen to music outside and hear the ocean inside. He came in when she was hunting for her father's brandy, having read somewhere that women drank brandy when they sat up late. A tall skinny man with a scraggly mustache and not much to say.

"Every cunt needs a fuck."

That was the one thing she didn't tell the police. It didn't matter anyway: they never found him.

Well, what do you know, Alex thinks through the Bowie. A name change and eight thousand baths and vomits later I'm still the same person. "I don't want to." Christ, I don't want to be.

Alex turns off the stereo and goes into her bathroom. She runs cold water over her index and middle fingers, sticks them down her throat, and vomits up half an ice-cream sundae and an apple.

The ride to the police station had been almost funny. Her father had put his old trench coat around her, her mother had combed her hair, Nicole had told her the movie was terrible. Each member of her family had one thing to say and repeated it endlessly.

"I'll kill the bastard," her father growled, hunched over the wheel.

"Please, dear, you're upsetting Alexandria; you need to be thinking about her now."

Her little sister sat in the back whispering, "Did he hurt you, Alexandria? Alexandria, did it hurt?"

She'd looked at her sister and tried to block out the cacophony coming from the front seat.

"Nicole," she said. "No more Alexandria. It's Alex."

"But why? Did he hurt you, did it hurt, Alexandria?"

"Alex," Alex said firmly.

"Alex," her sister whispered, "did he hurt you?"

I should have learned from Nicole, Alex thinks, pressing her cheek against the cool tile wall of the bathroom. A name change doesn't take you away from what you are. Does anything?

The next morning she has brunch with Edward.

"You missed Her Majesty's party," Edward says, throwing a waxed menu on the table. "How brave of you."

"No, not brave, just a lousy date." They are at Breadmans. Waitresses in denim miniskirts carry heavy trays and race between wide wooden tables. Graduate students bring their children here and ignore the mess they make with ketchup and scrambled eggs; fraternity boys come in groups to eat greasy sandwiches and kid each other over how good it was the night before. It is the only place in town with tables you can spread all of the Sunday *New York Times* over and still have room for plates. It is the place to be on a Sunday morning. Edward used to take Caroline here after a night of lovemaking. Being with him now, after he has spent the night, she assumes, fucking Susan, makes Alex feel traitorous.

"James Harrington?"

"Yes."

"So, what happened?"

"What else? He wanted to fuck, I didn't. He left, I went to sleep."

Edward orders for them both and plays with the cream holder. "We've had this conversation more times than I can remember, Alex."

She smiles. "One after every date?"

"You don't like him?"

"I don't know. I hardly know him." She separates the Sweet'n Low packets from the sugar. "What's the point, Edward? I panicked all afternoon about how I looked, where to go, what to say, and for what? To feel lousy about myself because I won't give some egomaniac a tumble?"

"I don't know what to tell you, Alex. Dating is supposed to be fun, like sex."

She stares at him. Sex fun? Right.

"You want me to take you to the cocktail party my frat is having? I can introduce you to some guys."

"Oh, Edward, you're so sweet. I know you want to take Susan."

"Alex, I want you to be happy."

"Thanks, love. I'll be happy when I get some food."

"I'm serious, Alex."

"Edward, go with Susan. You'll have a better time."

"Don't be silly. You are the best time in town."

She narrows her eyes and crosses her arms across her chest.

"Look, Alex, I want to take you. I would have fun."

She continues to stare him down. It's possible he is telling the truth, but still...

"Okay. I'll take Susan."

Alex laughs. "That was tough wasn't it? I'm sure she'll make a good impression on all the bros."

"No, Alex. You would make an impression, Susan will fit in."

She looks around the noisy restaurant. It seems as if all of Chapel Hill is here or waiting to get in. Is she hallucinating, or do all the men look like James Harrington? Fit in. Right.

5◊

Football Saturday

It has been a bad week. Alex did have a quiz on Wednesday, which, because she slept through her Monday class and did not call Caroline, she was completely unprepared for. Ten percent of her grade. F.

Alex lies in bed now, looking at the books she stacked neatly on her desk. She spent most of last night—another dateless Friday—arranging and rearranging them, before succumbing to the lure of Fitzgerald's short stories. Today she should get up, run, and then lock herself in the library. She groans, knowing that all she will do today is maybe run.

In three hours Alex is going to a football game, the first one in her life. Caroline has coerced her and Penelope into going, and they have spent the week cramming for this.

"What's a punt?"

"A kick."

"A down?"

"A play, and you have four for each ten yards."

She gets out of bed and looks in her closet. She has heard that people really do themselves up for these things. Nylons and dresses. No way. She ate a box and a half of chocolate-chip cookies last night, and while they are no longer inside of her, she is not even going to risk seeing if her stockings fit. Anyway, the radio said it was going to be eighty-two degrees.

Penelope will be happy. She will get a tan.

"I don't believe all these people," Penelope keeps saying. Around them mill hundreds, maybe thousands, of people—alumni, parents, and students. They all look excited and happy. People who only see each other on these Saturdays call "How you doin'?" as they pass. The campus has been invaded by parents intent on showing their children where they went to school and where they fully expect their offspring to go. Parking, always limited, has become a nightmare. People are eating chicken out of straw baskets from the trunks of their cars.

"That's called tailgating," Caroline explains. "It's a type of picnic. This is a very big social event, girls."

"Christ, there are more cops here than there are at a Bowie concert."

"Those aren't cops, Alex. Those are the people who

control parking and direct traffic. Everyone wants to park near the stadium."

"Look at that BMW," Alex says, pointing to a shiny gray car. "Can you imagine driving a BMW to a football game?"

"That's a Mercedes," Caroline says. "Not a BMW."

"It's going to be one of those days," Alex says with disgust.

Penelope laughs. Lights a cigarette. She cannot believe the number of people here. All dressed as if they were going to church. She can see up the skirt of the woman in front of her; the slit is too far up the seam. It would never pass muster at home.

"How do you know where we're going?" asks Penelope. They have arrived at Stadium Drive, and the river of people is breaking down into streams, each heading to a different gate opening.

Caroline shows her the ticket. "See those numbers? They tell us what section and row. We have good seats. Fifty-yard line."

"Oh, good," Alex says.

Penelope glares at her. Good what?

They do not get anything to drink. The stands sell only Coke, no Tab. Because it is out in the open, the stadium seems bigger than Madison Square Garden. Pine trees loom above the highest deck. They are sitting on benches of thin aluminum across from the box on the side that holds the board of trustees and other dignitaries. On the field are members of the marching band, cheerleaders, and baton twirlers in silky white and Carolina-blue leotards. People up and down the bleachers are balancing large pale blue plastic cups into which they will pour the alcoholic contents of flasks and Thermoses smuggled into the stadium.

"I've never seen so many blond women in my life," says Alex.

"What's wrong with blond?" Penelope inquires.

"Oh, you know what I mean. Women who are just blond. You're blond and . . . and . . ."

"An Amazon," Caroline supplies.

"Right."

Penelope lights another cigarette. The man next to her wearing a plaid shirt and a UNC hat leans over and says, "Would you mind putting that out? My girlfriend's allergic."

Penelope looks at Caroline.

"If someone asks, you have to put it out."

"For fuck's sake. You can smoke in the damn library, why not here?"

"Don't even say that word," Alex says.

"What?"

"Library. I'm so behind."

"Well, so am I," Caroline says. "Don't worry."

"Not as much as me. You dropped comp. lit."

"Really? How come?" Penelope asks.

"It was boring. Look, here comes the team."

About forty men in light blue come out followed by forty more in yellow. The crowd stands and cheers. Sits down again.

"Who are we playing?" Penelope asks.

"Georgia Tech."

"It was not boring," Alex says, staring at Caroline, having completely ignored the team's entrance. "Dr. Jordan is a great teacher."

"I disagree. Watch, they're going to kick off."

"Well, he's beautiful."

"Oh, Alex. I've seen him, and I don't think so," Penelope says.

"But you should see him talk about Dante. He gets this glow."

The crowd around them erupts. Penelope turns to the field.

"What happened?"

"We have the ball."

"Of course we do," Penelope says. "It's our ball."

"Oh, God," Caroline says. "Now look, see those two orange posts on the side of the field? We have four plays to move the ball beyond the ten yards those posts mark off."

"What if we don't?" Alex asks, watching four yellow men jump a blue one.

"They get the ball."

"What do you mean they get it? Don't they have to take it from us?"

"No."

Penelope looks at the side of the field where the cheerleaders are jumping around and the mikeman is trying to get the crowd to cheer with him and is being ignored. Two of the female cheerleaders are black, sinewy, and sleek as they ricochet back and forth. She looks down at her pale arms and decides her tan has definitely faded. The male cheerleaders are ugly, but she would like to whisper into Caroline's ear, "Look at that guy's ass," only she doubts Caroline would hear her, so busy is she explaining this dumb game to Alex. The players don't seem to run very far, but they are doing something involving the ball, which she has lost sight of.

♦ ♦ ♦

Alex wishes she brought a pair of sunglasses with her. The sun's glare is like a piece of slightly opaque glass, and the game is hard enough to follow. The crowd is applauding a player limping off the field. One of his teammates runs in to take his place.

"I'll bet he's pissed," says Alex.

"I wish life were like that," Caroline answers.

"Like what?" Penelope snaps, joining in unexpectedly.

"If someone got hurt or screwed up, they could just be replaced, and once everything started up again you could hardly tell the difference."

She means Edward, Alex thinks, looking away from her friend and the game. Her eyes land on the baton twirlers. She cannot believe what she sees: eleven clones with tight asses and slender legs. She puts her hands under her rear and then slides them over the tops of her thighs. She looks back to the twirlers. They really look exactly alike; it upsets her to see what she covets on just anyone.

"We should make a name for those girls," she says to Penelope.

"What do you mean?" Penelope asks in a distracted manner. "Look at how many people are wearing dresses."

"Well, if we're Amazons, what are they?" Alex asks, scanning the crowd. She sees a familiar thin long back in a brown-striped shirt. It is Edward, and next to him is—

"Susan," she says aloud in surprise. She has answered her own question. Edward usually goes with his fraternity brothers to these things.

"Funny," says Penelope, "but I don't think that will do. Even Susan has to have more going for her than these dipshits."

"Well, what then?" Alex persists.

"So you want a name, huh? A term, a label."

"Yes."

Penelope shakes her head. "Alex, you only use a name to distinguish a group. There are so many girls like that in the world, one can hardly bother telling them apart."

Alex loves the way she says "hardly": rolling over the "r" and slipping into the "d."

"Do you guys want to watch or gossip?" Caroline asks. They are going to ruin her day if they keep talking about stupid girls.

"Gossip," Penelope and Alex say. Alex gives Caroline a hug.

"Oh, you smell good. What are you wearing?"

Caroline remembers the first time Edward watched her get ready for a party.

"It's funny," he said, "that as independent as you are, you put on perfume."

"I like how it smells," she said.

"No, I think you just can't fight that female instinct." He kissed her then, clouding the implication that independence was not a natural part of being female.

"The Givenchy Penelope bought me," Caroline replies to Alex.

"Can I borrow it sometime?"

"Yes, now watch. This is a good game. We just got our second field goal."

"How come you know so much about this?" Alex asks.

"When Carl was in Vietnam, Mom would turn the TV on early every Sunday and wait for the news. I would sit on my dad's lap, and he would explain the end of the football games to me, and we just started turning the TV on earlier and earlier."

Over the past few months, Caroline has found herself

thinking about Carl a great deal. When they told her he had died, she did not cry, thinking perhaps that death was just another extension of his being away from home. When they explained that it meant he would never come home, she did not speak to anyone for three weeks. They sent her, at age seven, to the only child psychiatrist in a five-hundred-mile radius, who explained that a severe loss often causes one to withdraw from one's immediate surroundings. Such a withdrawal can take months to occur, he said, or, as in Caroline's case, can happen immediately.

"Who has the ball?" Alex asks, and Caroline looks to the field to see. Explaining how Carolina got the ball from Georgia Tech, she sees Edward talking to Susan, probably explaining the same play she is. It drove him crazy that she could follow the game as well as he could.

"What's to talk about if we both understand?" he would ask when she'd get tickets.

"The immense subtlety of the play," she'd say, smiling.

Watching him now, from so far away, watching him so intensely that she has stopped speaking to Alex, Caroline realizes she should have walked away from her knowledge of the game as he walked away from her: quietly with little fanfare or messy emotion.

Caroline can tell that Alex's eyes have followed hers and are resting on Edward as well. She knows that Penelope has long since given up and is concentrating on getting some sun. She likes knowing what they are doing, without being sure, without caring if she is right. She looks back at Edward. She does not really know what he is doing, and she hopes that soon she will not care.

Carolina makes another touchdown. They are killing Georgia Tech. People begin banging on their seats; it sounds like a rainstorm or war planes flying overhead. Caroline closes her eyes.

Did it sound like this? she wonders silently. There will be no answer, of course, but she asks again. Was it like this, Carl, can I connect to you through a football game on a sunny day, or has the connection disintegrated entirely?

The roar stops. She opens her eyes. The kicking team is being sent in. On her left Penelope is smoking, and on her right Alex is biting her nails. I never want to leave them, she thinks, knowing of course that it will be impossible for them all to stay like this, in a row—separate yet connected.

6

Making It Fit

So this is what being on layout means, Susan thinks, holding a clear plastic ruler and a blue highlighting pen. Keeping straight how many picas per column makes her head swim; the only clear thought she can hold on to is that she doesn't want to be here. Work, Susan, work, she thinks. *The Tar Heel* rarely took on anyone midsemester, but the managing editor dates one of her sorority sisters. She sets the ruler against some copy and slices off the bottom line with a razor blade. It's crooked. Shit.

"I really admire Alex," Edward said one afternoon,

passing her the paper. "She saw that movie on one of the worst nights of her life, and yet she wrote a damn good review."

"I hate Woody Allen," Susan returned.

He laughed. "Alex said you would."

"Did she?" Susan tried to sound frosty and polite, the way Penelope would have.

"Don't get the back up," he said, squeezing her arm. "She just thinks Allen has a limited audience."

Susan took up the paper. "This is no big deal," she said, unable to defend her distaste for Allen. "Anyone can write for this rag."

"No, anyone cannot. Alex can, and Penelope would if she weren't so involved with the International Center. You should do something, Susan. You'd have fun."

Well, fun was not something she was having. Fun would be lying on the roof getting a tan. She'd read somewhere that in the Victorian age a mistress adopted her lover's drink and brand of cigarette. She wishes things were still that simple.

In the outer room, at the editor-in-chief's desk, Alex is talking to her editor.

"I didn't know Steve was short-handed," she says.

"What do you mean?" asks Alicia, looking up from her edit.

"I saw Susan Simmons working in backshop."

"Oh, yeah. Well, Steve says she really wants to get involved, and she's nice, so I said go ahead."

"Nice! She's a sycophant."

"I didn't know you knew her."

"I don't," Alex says.

"You are weird."

"I know." Alex returns to the arts desk. She looks at her copy and pulls it out of the typewriter. Maybe she'd like Susan more if the girl ever spoke above a whisper. Alex knows some people on campus think she herself is too loud, but at least no one has to strain to hear her.

A loud voice from the office's entrance calls, "Alex!!" It is Penelope, who never has any trouble getting people to listen. She has come to get Alex for her daily four o'clock break.

"Be back soon," Alex tells Alicia, collecting her stuff.

"They put too much ice in these," says Penelope, sticking her tongue in the red paper cup of Tab. She is disinterestedly listening to Alex bad-mouth Cristen, who seems to have borrowed a sweater without permission.

"I mean, my God, if I did that, she'd throw me out. Her boyfriend will probably drool all over it when he gives her a hickey. They have such a juvenile relationship."

"Um." Penelope drinks her Tab and looks weary.

"I'd move out, but she might off herself. You don't know what it's like."

"You're right." Penelope shrugs on her jacket. "It's always too cold in here. Listen, have you seen Caroline lately?"

"Uh-uh. I was just going to ask you that—as soon as I got off my Cristen hobby horse."

"She hasn't been in your class, either?"

"No. I wish she would come. She takes much better notes than I do. We have a major midterm tomorrow that I need to get an A on, but I keep spacing out during the lectures."

"Damn. I've left a hundred messages with her roommate, but you know that doesn't mean a thing."

Alex knows. Caroline lives on South Campus, a collection of four dorms a good twenty-minute walk from the Pit. They'd been built when the university was forced to admit black students, and despite recent protests against de facto segregation, South Campus was still the home for most black students segregated from the rest of campus. Caroline roomed with a woman she called "the only South Campus Sorority Sue." The only thing Caroline and S.C.S.S., as Alex called her, had in common was that they both smoked. At any rate Caroline rarely got her messages, or for that matter rarely took very clear ones for S.C.S.S.

"What do you need her for?" Alex asks, crunching some ice.

"Do you know that means you're sexually frustrated?"

"So I've heard."

"I don't know how you could have told James no. How long are you planning on staying intact?"

"I'm not," are the words on the tip of Alex's tongue, but she decides to pass; this is not the time or place. Sometimes, sometimes I wish I could have a black "R" stamped on my forehead, like poor Hester, Alex thinks. Then everyone would leave her alone, hold her, comfort her, and understand her all at once.

"What do you need her for?" Alex repeats instead. Life can be made simple, if only by omission.

"I don't. I'm just worried. I haven't seen her since the game, and I think she's still pretty cut up over Edward. I'm sure they had a fight at my party. Of course I can't be certain." Here Penelope pauses coyly, which annoys Alex. "I was otherwise occupied."

"Yes, you could say that." Alex had been less than thrilled when Penelope told her she was involved with a homosexual, but things seem to be going okay for Miss

Samms. So far. "Listen," she says, "someone on the paper is writing a story about AIDS on campuses. I thought only people in New York and San Francisco got it, but it supposedly is very widespread."

"So?"

"So, try not to be 'otherwise occupied' with a gay man who may kill you with disease. They recommend that you use a rubber."

"I have a brand-new diaphragm."

"We're not talking about pregnancy here, we're talking about disease."

"Men won't use them anyway. They say it's like coming in a glove. Or taking a shower in a raincoat."

"Well, they have a nerve. I am talking about your life, not their sexual pleasure."

"Darling, I would love it if Colin and I actually *did* anything that could give me AIDS, but so far..."

"Penelope, I'm being serious. If you sleep with him, it could kill you."

"Oh, Lord, Alex. So I'll die. You'll probably die, too, from all that vomiting."

"I haven't done it in a day and a half," Alex says, neglecting to add she hasn't had anything to eat, either. That's one way to quit, but it won't last.

"Good."

They stare at each other, smile.

"I wonder where she is," Alex says.

"Who?"

"Caroline. The one you're dying to get hold of."

"I'm not dying to get hold of her," Penelope says. "She's my friend, and I'm concerned."

"Yes, I'm sure," Alex says, wondering if Penelope needs Caroline's notes as badly as she herself does.

"What's that mean?"

"Nothing. Just that I'm sure. Edward," Alex calls to his passing figure.

He smiles, checks his watch, and then brings a chair to their table. Edward is always running late and always checks the time before doing anything. It drives Alex crazy. "I'm not something you can just squeeze in when it fits," she snapped to him once. "I take a lot of time and trouble, but"—here she paused and smiled flirtatiously—"but I'm really worth it." He told her she was right, she is worth it, but he still checks his watch.

"Hullo, girls."

Penelope nods, but Alex leans forward and says intently, "Edward, how old am I?"

"Nineteen."

"Almost twenty. How old is Penelope?"

By now he has caught on. "Sorry," he says. "Hello... Alex. 'Hello, women' sounds too ridiculous. Will you settle for 'ladies'?"

"Done," she says brightly. It's nice when he's agreeable.

"Have you been to the office?" he asks.

Alex nods. Penelope crunches some ice, making her friend laugh.

"Sorry, Alex. That was just plain frustration, no special kind."

"Huh?"

"Nothing, Edward," they both say, and laugh.

"Tell me," he says.

Penelope reaches over and pats his arm. "You can't take it personally, darling. It's an Amazon joke. No men allowed."

Alex looks at his face and feels guilty. He is their best friend—outside of Caroline. He puts up with so much:

like the time she talked for two hours about a scene from *Lawrence of Arabia* without being stoned or aware he hadn't seen the film; when Penelope asked him if she looked like a fag hag and then had to explain what one was; sleeping with Caroline, who probably never let him forget that she was smarter than he was. And they keep so much from him, all the little day-to-day things that go with Tab and keep them tied to each other. Of course, he is sleeping with Susan now; perhaps he deserves to be shut out of their lives. "Did you see Susan there?" he asks, as if reading her mind.

"Oh, yes. A real trooper, she is."

"Alexandria, can't you be nice?"

"Tried it once. It didn't agree with my temperament."

Penelope laughs. "Oh, darling," she says.

"I'll say this about you, Alex," Edward says, "you usually vocalize all the nasty things I'm thinking so that I don't have to."

"Are you thinking nasty things about Susan?" Penelope asks politely.

"No."

"You should be," Alex says.

Edward sighs, tries again. "Alex, there's a guy in my philosophy class who likes you. I told him what a bitch you are, but he says he'll risk it."

"Who is it?" This from both women.

"Simon Reels. You met him at my house a couple of weeks ago. You guys were sunbathing."

Alex remembers. A tall boy with curly dark hair. She'd come inside to get Penelope a glass of water wearing only a Lycra one-piece black Speedo and a silver star in her left ear.

"Which are you?" he asked.

"Excuse me?" she said.

He pointed at her earring. "You know—'Left is right, right is wrong,' or something like that."

She turned to the sink to get water, hoping her ass looked tight, her legs slender. She didn't say anything to him.

"Ugh," says Penelope now. "He belongs to the DKE fraternity. Tell him she said forget it."

"Block that remark," says Alex. "You tell him I say yes to anyone who asks. I'm desperate. And hopeful."

"Well, girls—uh, ladies, it's been real, see you soon."

Penelope watches Edward leave and then hisses, "Alexandria, are you nuts? You don't want to lose it to Simon Reels. He's a southerner."

"Why are you so anxious for me to lose it? If I recall correctly, your first time was not so great. 'He just rolled over and went to sleep, and I kept thinking, This is it?' I believe I'm quoting."

"Yes, darling, but he was fifty-one, a famous author who thought he was doing me a big favor. I wanted the experience. You, my dear, need desperately to get it over with."

Alex stands up. "Shut up, will you. Anyway, I'm holding out for my 'innocent man.'"

"Vomiting won't kill you, Alex. Dreaming will."

There is a song by Billy Joel on a record of Cristen's that Alex wore out by playing it so much. When she saw the thinned grooves, Alex called Penelope in a panic and told her that they had to drive to Raleigh to the all-night Record Bar to replace the album before Cristen came back from her boyfriend's.

Penelope laughed. "Okay, Alexandria. What record is it?"

"'An Innocent Man.'"

"Billy Joel!" Penelope screeched. "Haven't you got any taste? Not only is he hideous, he can't sing."

"It's this one song. It gives me hope."

In the car she tried to explain more. "Listen," she said, quoting, "I know you're only protecting yourself because of someone else who hurt you, but I can find out what happened and fix where it all began. I am an innocent man."

"That's the dumbest thing I've ever heard," Penelope said, laughing so hard she almost ran off the road.

"You don't understand," Alex protested. "It's all I want from a man. Not stunning looks, brilliance, or even money. I just want him to come and say this to me and mean it."

Penelope laughed some more, but the midnight ride had bonded the two, not just against Cristen and her record fetishes, but against abusive men, and the memory of the ride always gave them something to smile at.

"Let me find out how this all began/I'll stop the heartache if I can/Because I am an innocent man," Alex hums on her way out of the Student Union.

7.

Where Caroline Is

Caroline is sitting in a bar, nursing a Scotch. It occurs to her that she should be at the library tonight studying for her midterm tomorrow, that she doesn't know the name of the establishment she is frequenting, and that she is probably drunk. This is one of those times I wish I were Penelope, she thinks. Penelope becomes giggly, vivacious, and flirty when drunk, without ever resembling a Sorority Sue. Caroline becomes somber, serious, and sad.

She remembers where she is now—O'Grady's, where on November third, her freshman year, a group went after a rally commemorating the anniversary of the Greensboro slaying, where several Klansmen murdered some Communist party members. She had thought then that radical politics could become her forte. She had been wrong. She asks the bartender for another drink and is surprised when a five-dollar bill appears in front of her face.

"I'll get that, pretty lady," says a smooth southern drawl.

Caroline turns and looks at the sharp, angular face of a stranger. Wait a minute. She has seen him on campus, talking in the Pit, even. Trying to outshout the preacher. What about? Divestment? She can't remember; she spends all her time in the Pit listening to Alex and Penelope.

"Thank you," she says.

"My name is Bob," he tells her. "Live around here?"

"Not really," she says, figuring he must be a graduate student. A lot of them live in Durham because the rent is cheaper and commute to Chapel Hill for class. The bartender has placed another Scotch in front of her and Caroline is trying to concentrate on how this will be her last one.

"You at the university?"

She nods. Isn't everyone?

"That's what I thought. I was sitting back there...." Here he swivels her stool and points it toward the deep recesses of the bar and then swivels it back. "I was sitting back there watching you, and I said to myself, That's a university girl, or I haven't got the longest dick in Durham."

Caroline tries to focus on him. She is not sure she heard right; she's still dizzy from swiveling on the stool. A voice in the back of her head says that Alex would inform

Bob that Durham is a small town, so big deal. She shakes her head.

"You don't believe me?" Bob asks.

"No, I believe you." She takes her car keys out. "Thanks for the drink."

"Hey, wait, pretty lady. I wouldn't have bought you a drink if I knew you were driving. I teach French. I'm a responsible person."

"You sound a little drunk to me," she says.

"A drunk man is more clear-headed than a drunk woman," he replies. "You better let me get you home, pretty girl."

Pretty girl. What is it Alex and Penelope call Susan? She can't remember, it's too hard to concentrate. Pretty girl, huh? She hands the man her keys.

Cristen comes to Alex's bedroom with the phone in her hand.

"For you," she says, and then stands in the doorway, the way Dr. Rust used to when Alexandria was in high school.

"Hello?" Alex says, looking at her clock. It is 2:40 A.M.

"Alex?"

"Yes? Who is this?"

"It's Caroline. Alex, I'm in a lot of trouble. I need someone to pick me up and two hundred dollars."

"Where the hell are you?"

"Police station on Airport Road. Didn't Cristen say?"

"No, no, she didn't." Alex begins to crawl out of bed. She wishes she didn't feel so fat; her hips hurt, and if she were thin, she'd be able to deal with this better.

"How soon can you get here?"

"Did your car break down?" Alex asks.

"No, I've got a DUI." Caroline suddenly begins to cry, something Alex has never heard. "Alex, please hurry."

"I'll be right there," Alex says, and hangs up. There is a tingly feeling in her throat, and she hopes there's a milk product in the house. "Cristen, will you call Penelope and tell her to come pick me up?"

"I can take you," Cristen says as Alex stumbles to the kitchen.

"Thanks, but I think it would be better this way. God, I wish I had my license." Alex takes a coffee yogurt from the icebox. I'm the only one in the world, she thinks, gulping it down, who eats more, instead of less, to be thin.

She goes to the bathroom, vomits, washes her face, and then gets dressed. Now her jeans fit; two minutes ago, they wouldn't have. She really believes that.

"Penelope's just driven up," says Cristen, who's been watching by the window and who will certainly stay there until Alex returns.

Alex grabs her checkbook, keys, and passport for ID. "Sorry she woke you," she tells Cristen, and slams the door.

"A DUI?" Penelope asks, incredulous as Alex gets into the car.

"That's what she said. I'm glad my dad just cabled money."

Penelope laughs. Alex has a system. She calls her father at his office, says, "Can you call me back? I can't afford this call," and then hangs up. Her father cables money to Alex's Chapel Hill account and then calls her back. They never discuss it; but the plan is foolproof and makes a good story.

"I wonder where she was coming from," Penelope says

when they pull into the police parking lot.

"God knows."

When they enter the police station, Alex, for the first time in two years, wants to retch for reasons unrelated to food. Caroline is sitting on a chair, and she has two black eyes.

"I'll file brutality charges," Alex hisses.

"Don't be daft. That's her mascara."

Alexandria hugs Caroline without speaking.

"Everything will be okay," Penelope says tonelessly. Up this close, Alex sees Penelope was wrong; it is not mascara.

"I'm here with bail," Alex tells the officer sitting at the desk, viewing them impassively. "Sgt. Toomey," reads his black badge, in carved white lettering.

"Well, well, I've worked the dead man's shift for five years, but I can't remember the last time two *girls* came to bail anyone out of trouble. Usually it's a parent or boyfriend."

Alex stares at him. "Could I just pay the bail, please?"

"It's not bail exactly, ma'am. You won't be getting it back. It's a fine."

"But she hasn't even been to court yet."

"She will. I've already pulled her license, and, ma'am, the money's not the fine they're going to slap on her for a DUI. It's for towing her car."

"Her car?" Penelope inquires, sounding terribly BBC.

"I ran into a tree," Caroline says, speaking for the first time.

At least she sounds the same, Alex thinks. She makes no sense, but she sounds the same.

"She ran into a tree? Is that how she hurt her face?" Penelope has evidently decided that Sergeant Toomey is a better spokesman for Caroline than Caroline is.

"She ran off the road avoiding the arresting officer." He stops here and tilts his chair back. "Your friend maintains that earlier this evening a man tried to force her into sexual relations and when she refused blackened both her eyes."

Alex drops to her knees and puts both arms around Caroline. "Is that true? Did someone try and rape you?"

"Yes. I've been telling him that." Caroline begins to cry again, tiny trickles of water forcing themselves out of her swollen eyes. "That I was running from *him,* not the police. I knew I'd been drinking too much to drive, but I had no other way of escaping."

"Are you looking for the rapist?" Alex asks quietly.

"Alleged rapist," Sergeant Toomey corrects with a grin. He looks at Penelope. "You look like one of those singers on MTV," he says, pointing at her spiky hair.

"Has she had a medical exam?" Alex snaps.

His grin disappears. "No."

"Then how the fuck do you know if it's alleged or not?"

"Now, ma'am, there's no need for obscenity."

"There isn't? You've arrested a rape victim, you're charging her two hundred dollars for towing the vehicle she was using to escape, you haven't gotten her to a doctor, and her attacker's running loose. If there was ever a time to say fuck and to say it loud, I would say it's now."

Penelope is getting scared. "Alex, calm down." She has never seen either friend lose control, and to have them both suddenly fall apart is not doing wonders for her sanity.

"I will not calm down. We have to get to student health. Caroline needs a DES."

"No, I don't, Alex. He never got in."

"What's a DES?" Penelope is beginning to lose her grip. Alex seems just too familiar and at ease with this whole scene.

"A morning-after pill." Alex turns back to Caroline. "Are you sure? It's okay, you can tell me."

"How the hell do you know about DESs?" Penelope is not entirely sure she wants an answer. I mean, enough is enough, she thinks, scraping the polish off a nail.

For the first time Caroline smiles. "Yes, I'm sure. And thanks, I know I can tell you. I just don't want to talk about it. It was horrible."

Penelope sees that despite her businesslike manner, Alex is able to relate a bit too well to Caroline emotionally. What is going on?

"Who do I make the check out to?" Alex asks the sergeant.

"City of Chapel Hill," he tells her.

Penelope scratches wanly at her nail polish and watches Alex write and Caroline take a deep, relieved breath. Despite her friends' different actions, Penelope senses a bond between them she had not known existed. She wishes for her own sake and Alex's that it didn't.

"New York, huh?" he asks, examining her passport. "It figures."

"Yes, and I'm sure that answers all your questions about my behavior."

"Yup. Nice photo," he adds, pushing the small blue book back.

"Thank you," she says.

In the car Alex turns to the backseat, where Caroline is stretched out. "We're going to take you to Penelope's," she informs her.

"We are?" Penelope says.

"Fine," says Caroline.

"Yes, we are," says Alexandria.

"I want to know what happened," Penelope says. Alex punches her thigh. "However, it can wait."

"Penelope, I'm sorry. I just don't want to talk. Are you mad at me?"

"Mad? No, not mad, but concerned." About both of you, she thinks, looking at Alex's profile. Caroline and Alex seem to be sharing something. She is usually so in tune to their feelings. Why are they shutting her out from this?

At the house, Penelope makes tea while Alex puts sheets on the couch and Caroline goes to the bathroom.

"There's witch hazel in the cabinet," she calls to Caroline when taking the pot and three cups into the living room.

"She's so lucky, she's so damn lucky she got away. It's very hard to do. Maybe he was drunk, too, or didn't sneak up on her," Alex says, curling up on Penelope's favorite chair. She is staring into space, not looking at the walls around her but at some inner picture. Though her body seems calm, she keeps opening and closing her hands in a horribly jerky manner. It is so clear that Alex is not talking or thinking about what has happened to Caroline, so Penelope just sits on the floor and doesn't say anything until Caroline comes out.

"Here," she says, passing a mug of tea. She is curious about what happened, but she is also annoyed. Why did Caroline call Alex, who doesn't have a car? And has Caroline guessed that Alex, too, has been a rape victim, or did she know, and regardless, why hasn't Alex ever told her?

She looks at Caroline's bluish eyes. "I have a really neat pair of glasses you can borrow till the swelling goes down," she says. "No one has to know. They'll think you're pulling a Michael Jackson."

"Do you have a glove?" asks Caroline, and smiles lamely.

Alex puts down her tea. "What happened, Caroline? Do you want to tell us?"

Caroline laughs. "What didn't happen?" she returns.

"Look on the bright side," Penelope interjects. "For once you can be glad you're not a Bullfoot. They'd have to take the scholarship away. DUI's a criminal offense."

"That's comforting," Caroline says.

Penelope takes the teapot to the kitchen. She does not return.

"You want to lie down?" Alex asks. Take a bath? she thinks.

Caroline gets between the sheets on the couch and reaches for Alexandria's hand. "Thank you," she says. "Thank you for believing me. But can you believe that all I wanted tonight was to feel pretty again?"

"No crime in that," Alex whispers. "But you're still pretty to me."

And it's true. At no time has Caroline ever seemed more beautiful to Alex. You lucky bitch, she thinks. You got away.

After Alex has gone and Penelope has said a curt good-night and stomped upstairs, Caroline lies looking at the white paint peeling off the ceiling and listening to the breeze move through the trees by the open window. She decides she will never let anyone buy her a drink again.

Her whole body aches from fear and hate. When she finally falls asleep, it's only to dream. She's riding in her car with Bob driving about ninety miles an hour. Edward appears in the backseat and says, "If you fuck this guy, I can guarantee that tomorrow you'll wake up a different person."

The car is flying now, and right before they crash into the Golden Gate Bridge, which has suddenly appeared, Edward adds, "One more thing. I get to watch."

She wakes afraid, knowing that she would have told him yes, he could watch, and if it were only true, then she could be looking forward to tomorrow.

8◇

Penelope Plans

The phone rings six times before Penelope answers. She is hoping it is Colin, and if it is, she doesn't want to seem too anxious. She knows it can't be Alex because she just finished talking with her, and they managed to speak for thirty minutes without once mentioning rape, Caroline's or Alex's, why Alex has never told her, or how Caroline is doing. Penelope considers this quite a feat and thinks she should be rewarded, but it isn't Colin, just someone for her housemate Nancy. She sighs and goes back to her room. She is sitting in the middle of her floor, surrounded by fashion magazines, staring at the blank wall opposite her bed. She has a pair of scissors and an idea of making a collage. She pulls an old *Mademoiselle* toward her. Christie Brinkley smiles at her. Christie Brinkley is married to Alex's favorite singer, Billy Joel. On Penelope's left is a *Vogue* with Jerry Hall on the cover. Jerry Hall dates Mick Jagger. Patti Hansen married Keith Richards. When Penelope was in grade school, before the move to Paris happened, the Stones got busted in the States for some drug possession charge. She'd followed the story in all the Fleet Street papers she could buy. Her father found a stack of them under her bed and had a fit.

"Do I need to remind you that this is the same rag that periodically refers to me as king of the vacuum bags?" he shouted, holding a copy of the *Daily Mirror,* which showed Keith trying to cover his face with a handkerchief.

"Kingpin, not king," Penelope whispered.

"Get rid of them," he ordered.

I would kill or die to screw a Rolling Stone, Penelope thinks now. She laughs at herself. Face it. She would kill or die to screw anyone. Maybe this collage isn't such a great idea. If she ever gets Colin back to bed, she doesn't want him looking at the wall and then her. She knows who will come off looking bad.

"Cross that bridge when we get to it, old girl," she says aloud.

The phone rings again. Miracle of miracles it is Colin, wanting to know if, after rehearsal, she wants to meet him and the cast of the play he's in. She says yes and tears back to her room. She hasn't a bleeding thing to wear. Wait a minute. Bright blue miniskirt, lacy white top, that should do it. Objectively Penelope knows she looks good. She also knows she could not make a hundred thousand dollars a year off how she looks, like half the rock world's female consorts. Too bad, she tells the mirror. Lucky for me Colin's not a rock star. Yeah, he's queer instead, says a voice. Shut up, Penelope tells it. She's happy, she's ready, she's gone.

They meet at Pyewacket, an upscale health food restaurant with soft brown carpeting and cool still air. Fern plants hang from the windows, and one can order hot carob drink or leafy green salad. To her amusement, Greg Neals is there.

"Hello, lovey," he says, trying to kiss her cheek.

His eyes run over her body the way his hands did so long ago, and she forces herself to remember that he looks this way at every woman he encounters. She is not special to him, so she leans away from Greg and kisses Colin.

"Well," Greg says, "I have to be going. Great rehearsal everyone. See you all tomorrow." He fixes his eyes on Penelope for a moment before leaving.

Penelope orders white wine, knowing that this is what people drink after play rehearsal.

Penelope likes theater people. She likes knowing that Karin Felix gets all the leads because she looks like the director's daughter and is a safe way of satisfying his hang-up. Despite her behavior toward him, she is fascinated by tales of Greg Neals, who does indeed screw anything that walks. Beautiful men who do that have a lot of power, because people want them more, as a challenge, out of curiosity, whatever. Beautiful women who do it do not have a lot of power; they have a lot of what Penelope's mother calls "reputation." Penelope doesn't care. She doesn't even want to think about women who screw everything that walks. That would be depressing.

The waitress who is serving them looks mad, as if she knows she's going to get stiffed. And she will, not out of spite, but because everyone's broke. Penelope puts a cigarette in her mouth, and Colin lights it. She smiles at him.

"You bored?" he asks.

"No, not at all."

"Good." He smiles, and she thinks, not for the first time, that if she ever gets to heaven, she's going to give it to God for wasting all those looks on a homo.

"I disagree." Colin is interrupting a pale blond man who dangerously resembles Conrad. "There's no way Sanford can beat him. The entire eastern Carolina good old boy network is behind Broyhill. I hope I'm wrong, but I doubt it."

"Yeah, you're right," says a girl with hair down to her ass. "Even the governor is supporting Broyhill."

"What do you mean, 'even'?" Colin asks. "Martin is a Republican. It's in his best interests to have Broyhill win. They did an edit on the race this morning in the *New York Times.*"

Penelope is astonished. She has heard (through Alex, who has a lot of gay friends on the paper) that the running joke about Colin is "beautiful house, too bad nobody's home." Doesn't sound so dumb to me, Penelope thinks. She herself never reads the *Times*—the articles are badly laid out and too long.

"All those rags will spoil you for the really good stuff, Penelope," she remembers her father saying. Too damn bad, Daddy.

"How's the play going?" she asks to the table, and is bombarded with "terrible," "so-so," and "great."

Everyone laughs. "It's still too early to tell," Colin says.

"We open right after fall break," says the girl with the hair.

"It will be too early then," the blond boy says.

Colin laughs. "It would help if we didn't hate the director," he says.

"I don't hate the director, I hate Karin Felix."

"No, Gina, you just hate that you don't look like her. Then you would get to be Maggie instead of the horrible sister-in-law," Colin says.

"Who's doing the Paul Newman role?" Penelope asks.

"Greg," says Colin. He himself has been cast against type and is playing Brick's ugly, envious brother. What a waste of looks, Penelope thinks. She read the play last term and felt such empathy for Maggie, who could not break the bond her husband held with another man. Men who love each other are so alluring.

"Anyway," Gina says, "maybe I don't hate Karin Felix, but I do hate Greg Neals."

"Why?" Penelope asks.

"Why does any woman hate Greg?" the Conrad blond asks.

Penelope shrugs. She does not hate Greg, still enjoys the fact that for a week last semester, when he could have had anyone, he chose her. The clean glass windows have turned into mirrors as night presses against the restaurant. She likes how most of her neck is visible between the top of her shirt and the bottom of her hair. She studies Gina, who is what Alex would call pretty: small, delicate, and thin. She is happy to be grouped with this woman as "one of Greg Neals's girls."

"It's kind of late," Colin says to her. "Let's go." They excuse themselves and dash for Penelope's car. It has begun to rain.

"If I had known then what I know now about Chapel Hill weather, I would never have left Paris."

"Uh, Penelope, I live in the other direction."

Obligingly she makes a U-turn. Maybe he's going to ask me up, she thinks. But he doesn't. He kisses her cheek, gets out, says he'll call her.

To her chagrin Penelope finds she is humming "An Innocent Man" on her way home.

In the kitchen she mixes a bowl of flour and water—a nursery school recipe for paste—and goes upstairs to finish her collage. When the last picture is up she surveys her work and then leans against it, looking at her poster of the Rolling Stones.

I will do it, she thinks fiercely. I will lose twenty pounds and become a famous model and screw Mick Jagger's brains out. And then, then I will never have any man problems again.

As she falls into bed, she hears the voice say, And then, then you will be dead. Penelope puts a pillow over her head and in a muffled voice says, "Screw you," to her empty room. Great. She could team up with Joan of Arc: Joan heard voices, and Penelope speaks to them. I'm coming for you, Mick, she thinks. But not out loud.

9

Picks and Pans

"It's true," Edward repeats. "Penelope and Alexandria would like to look just like you."

Susan has just gotten out of bed and is wearing a pair of cotton briefs and a T-shirt. She looks down at her skinny legs and flat chest. She thinks of Penelope's sleek, curvy body and Alexandria's earrings and tells Edward, "You're from hunger."

"All right," he says, lying back down. Edward does not have an eight o'clock class. "Don't believe me. But you have no reason to be afraid of them. They're nice people."

Susan pulls on her jeans. Maybe she shouldn't have told

him, but then men always like to hear how easily intimidated you are, and Susan believes you should tell men what they like to hear.

"Give them a chance," Edward continues. "They're just a little reserved, and rather caught up in themselves."

"Is it important to you?" Susan asks cautiously. She doesn't want to venture into the lion's den without having it pay off.

"Not at all," he says, eyes closed. "But it seems to be important to you."

She's surprised. He's right, it is important to her—not because of him, but because of her. How odd, she thinks. How odd that I should want to be a part of something related to Edward because I want it, not because he does.

This has never happened to her before.

Coming out of her eight o'clock class (which she was late to, because Edward had hidden her top under his pillow), Susan sees Alexandria, Penelope, and Caroline sitting on what Susan has come to think of as "their steps." They are drinking coffee, smoking, and Penelope at least is laughing hysterically. With Edward's words in mind she decides to join them. Not even an old girlfriend can scare her. If they want to look like me, they must like something about me.

She bounds up the steps, and they all freeze. Alex holds her coffee cup to her lips, Penelope keeps her hands in her hair, and Caroline is adjusting her glasses.

"Um, Penelope, I just wanted to thank you for your party." Stupid, that was weeks ago.

"Were you there?" Penelope inquires politely.

"Oh, she was there," Caroline says.

"So you were. Which is more than I can say for you,

darling," Penelope says, tapping Alex on the shoulder.

Knighting her almost, Susan thinks. "Yes, I missed seeing you," Susan tells Alexandria.

"Did you?" Alex lowers her cup. She is the last to unfreeze, but the first to smile. "Well, then I'm doubly sorry. A lousy date kept me away."

Susan cannot tell if Alexandria is being sincere or bitchy. She lowers herself onto a nearby step. She is reminded of a quote by Patti Smith in one of her favorite books—the biography of Edie Sedgwick. "It wasn't a question of my wanting to be them—Edie and company—I just liked that they existed so I could look at them."

Alexandria and Penelope are a beautiful study in contrast. Caroline seems mainly preoccupied with her sunglasses.

Susan sees a boy walking toward the steps, staring at Alexandria. He stands in front of them a few moments. "Hi," Caroline says.

Very pointedly, Penelope says nothing.

He clears his voice. "Um, Alexandria, I'm Simon Reels, and . . ."

"Yes, I know. I remember seeing you at Edward's," she says. "Most people call me Alex."

He smiles back. "Um, my fraternity is having a party Saturday, and I was wondering if you'd like to go."

"Depends on the fraternity," she says, and the Amazons laugh. "Just kidding," she adds. "I'd love to."

"It's a cocktail party. Six o'clock?"

"That's fine. You want me to meet you there?"

"Oh, no. I'll pick you up. You live at Townhouse Apartments, right?"

"Yes."

"See you," he says, and walks away.

"Hallelujah!" Alex exults. "A date."

Susan looks up. What's so great about a date? Simon's cute, but not even a Bullfoot.

"I highly disapprove," Penelope says.

"Oh, shut up, Penelope," Caroline says.

Susan is surprised. She has heard from Edward that you cannot really talk to Penelope like that.

Alex looks at her watch. "Omigod," she says. "Gotta run. Susan, aren't you in this class, too?"

"Uh, me? Yes, yes, I am."

"Well, come on. We're going to be late."

Alex says good-bye to Penelope and Caroline, and she and Susan set off.

"Um, Alexandria?"

"Susan, didn't you hear me? I really prefer Alex."

"But Alexandria is so pretty," Susan returns. "N-not," she stammers on, "that Alex isn't, but..."

Alex laughs and puts her hand on Susan's arm. "It's okay. You're right, Alexandria is pretty, which is why I prefer Alex. You see, I'm not."

"I think you are."

"Well, thank you. However, you can't date me, and people who can don't think so."

My mother could date you, Susan thinks. She shakes her head disgustedly; she should never have agreed to go see her mom over fall break—she has lesbians on the brain.

"What about Simon? He must think so."

Alex laughs. "He'll be the second date I'll have this semester. And probably the last."

"Oh." Susan cannot think of what to say. So she just repeats, "I think you're pretty."

Alex stops outside the classroom door. "Oh, no, Susan.

You're pretty. And in many ways I wish I were, too, but *che sera, sera.* I have other things."

You have everything, Susan thinks. But she doesn't say anything. She just sits in her seat and thinks, As usual I can't think of a thing to say.

Caroline and Penelope sit in uncomfortable silence. They have not spoken very much since that night at the police station. Caroline knows from Alex that Penelope is having trouble with Colin. She wishes she could help.

"That was one of those times I wished I were you," she tells Penelope.

"You mean with Susan here? Why?"

"I would have stared her out of existence or thought up something truly horrible to say."

"Really, Caroline, I am not that much of a bitch."

Caroline looks up, shocked. How could Penelope so badly misunderstand what she meant as a compliment?

"I have to go to the library," Penelope says, gathering her papers. "I'll see you."

Like a man's "I'll call you," it sounds empty, lame, and ugly.

Caroline sits alone on the steps. She is sorry Penelope has left, but enormously grateful to Alex for taking Susan away.

Susan makes her think of Edward, Edward of Bob, and Bob of... she is not sure of what, but that as much as she doesn't want to discuss that night, she doesn't want to think about it. She pushes her sunglasses farther up her nose. They make the Pit look dark and gloomy, though she knows it is a beautiful day. The air smells like wet earth, the sky is streaked with pale clouds, and because it is the South it is still warm and comforting out, despite the dying leaves. For the first time, Caroline really studies the man trying to save her soul. No one listens to him, but he does not seem to realize this. In fact, he does not seem to realize anything—he is in a complete trance. There is an invisible sheet between him and his supposed audience. Caroline would like to build such a sheet around herself now, to shut out Susan, Edward, and Bob, but how could she do that without blocking out Alex and Penelope as well? If Penelope is going to push Caroline out of her life, fine and good. Caroline has little intention of willingly returning the favor.

After class, Alex decides that nothing she can do on campus—sit in the Pit, go to the library, work in the *Tar Heel* office—appeals to her. She starts toward Franklin Street; since it's too early for lunch, she knows it will be pretty empty, which is nice. From twelve on, Franklin Street can be just an extension of campus—the danger of running into someone lurks everywhere.

As Alex walks past the shops she smiles. Franklin Street makes such a valiant effort to have something for everyone: the stodgy Town and Country Shop, for those into tweeds; the Fireside, which makes a stab at selling weird and funky things, like Canal Jeans moved uptown. She got a really good pair of plastic exercise pants there once. Behind the McDonald's there's the Internationalist Bookstore, a place Alex keeps meaning to go and browse through. She stops at the corner of Columbia and Franklin. Once you cross Columbia and get past the Logos Bookstore ("closed on the Lord's day"), you get into the more bohemian part of Franklin: secondhand clothing stores; the Breadshop, where the women who give you your bagels are always barefoot and pregnant; health food restaurants and stores; and a musty bookshop, where everything is in disarray, like the attic Alex always wanted, but which the New York apartment and the beach house could never accommodate. You have to be in the mood to cross Columbia, and Alex knows she's not in it. She sits on the wall next to the Carolina Movie House and outside the Happy Store.

"Christ," her father said freshman year when they'd driven past this corner. "The 'Happy Store.' Christ. Just remember," he added, turning toward the backseat, "Alexandria, that for four years the South was a separate country."

"It's Alex," she whispered.

"What?"

"Yes, Daddy, I'll remember."

And she did. Each time she passed the damn place she remembered that her father couldn't remember what to call her.

"What do I want today?" she wonders aloud, walking past the theater. She studies the Carolina classics schedule. *Funny Girl.* I haven't seen this movie in three years, she thinks. Too long. She buys a ticket. Big-nosed and big-talented Barbra gets beautiful Omar Sharif and then loses him because he can't deal with her success—the story is one of Alex's favorites. She rarely goes to the Carolina classics—they play the same movie for a week, and there's never more than five people in the theater—because she thinks they're a poor substitute for the New York revival houses that she practically grew up in, but it'll do. Through Barbra's declaring that she's the biggest star, Alex can hear Susan saying, "I think you're pretty."

Lulled into the forgetfulness of a cool dark theater, by

the time the credits have rolled, Alex stops feeling bad for every nasty thought she's ever had about Edward's girl. She leaves the theater peaceful and healed, humming "People Who Need People," the movie's theme song, on the walk home.

Fall in Chapel Hill is lovely. The leaves turn color without ever losing the moisture of their green counterpoints.

Cristen is talking on the phone when Alex comes in.

"Hold on, Celia, here she is." Silently Cristen hands the phone over to Alex.

"Hey, Celia, how's the nunnery?"

"It's fine. How're the rednecks?"

This is how they remind each other that each disapproves of the other's choice of college.

"Listen, I'm calling to see if you've given any thought to coming here for fall break."

Fall break. That's soon. Until what Penelope refers to as "Caroline's incident," the three had planned to go to the mountains. In North Carolina people talk about the mountains the way Alex thinks people in Europe must refer to the "baths." She has always wanted to discover what magical qualities the mountains possess. It will have to wait. This term, she knows she's not going anywhere with Penelope and Caroline together. It's true they're talking to each other, but Penelope's abrupt behavior and disgust over Caroline's DUI looms over the three of them, like a cloud aspiring to be a tornado. She does not realize that what Penelope is really mad about is having to figure out for herself that Alex was also raped.

"Yeah. I'll come," she says.

"Good. I just need to start prepping my roommate now." Celia's roommate is an exchange student from Delphi whose phone bill exceeds four hundred dollars a month. She needs time to adjust to each curve the Western world throws her and then to discuss it with her parents.

"And you," Celia tells Alex, "are a definite curve."

Alex laughs, tells Celia when she'll arrive, and hangs up.

"You could come home with me," Cristen says. "Mom would love to see you."

"Oh, thanks, Cristen, but it's been a long time since I've had a chance to really talk to Celia, and I think she's going through a rough time. Jonesfeld's really tough."

"So's UNC," Cristen snaps.

"I know."

"Good. What are you going to tell Penelope and Caroline?"

"About what?"

"Not spending fall break with them."

Not really interested, Alex wonders how Cristen knows that was her plan. Maybe she's bugged her brain.

"I'll cross that bridge—"

"When you get to it." Cristen was all too familiar with the Rust family's favorite phrase.

"I'd really love it, Cristen, if you let me talk for myself."

"That," Cristen says with some satisfaction, "has never been a problem."

Alex lies down on the couch. She closes her eyes. She pretends to sleep until she's sure Cristen has left for her two o'clock class.

10

Courtship

Three hours before Simon is supposed to pick her up and two hours before she wants to leave the library, Alex finds herself walking through the mall, trying to match Penelope's energy and direction.

"Now it's a cocktail party at a very southern frat. You need to look very ladylike."

"Can't I just look like me? He asked a New Yorker out, after all, not a southerner."

Penelope stops short and pulls Alex in front of her. One of the round pillars holding the ceiling up is covered in small square mirrors.

"Look at yourself."

Alex looks.

"We need to put your hair up. It's too long and messy. Your earrings are longer and messier than your hair."

Alex is desperately trying to get a clear picture of herself, but the disjointed mirrors make it impossible.

"I suppose my body is long and messy, too," she says.

Penelope studies her friend critically. "Strong legs, no hips, small ass, great bust," she lists. "With the right clothes," she says, "you'll be beautiful."

"If I need to fit in, I'd better just be pretty."

"Oh, darling," Penelope says, "an Amazon is never merely pretty. Come along."

Susan can feel Edward's hand on her back, moving up and down, lingering at each vertebra. She has been napping between his musty sheets, with her head on his lumpy pillow. They were supposed to study this afternoon, but she knew they wouldn't. When she agrees to meet him at his house, they always wind up in bed. She doesn't really mind except that it hurts and takes so long. She knows from reading *Cosmopolitan* that having a lover who takes a long time is a good and rare thing. From *Mademoiselle,* she knows that it is normal for young women to experience pain during sex, and that with time and experience the pain leaves, and it begins to feel good. Susan gathers from Edward that Penelope loves sex. If she had the nerve, Susan would ask her why and maybe learn something.

"Do you want to go out tonight?" Edward whispers, checking to see if she is awake.

"Well, I am kind of hungry."

"How about a movie?"

"Sure."

"What do you want to see?"

"You pick," she says. She always lets him pick. From *Seventeen,* she knows this is a good thing to do.

"Alex, you have to choose one you like," Penelope says. They are in a small dressing room looking at six discarded outfits. Alex points to the purple skirt with green squares on it.

"Too loud," Penelope says.

"This one?"

"Too lacy. You'll look like you're going on a picnic."

"You pick. I really don't care. I refuse to get hyper about what to wear for a guy who's going to ask me to fuck and then take a walk when I say no."

"So say yes," Penelope says, holding up a black clingy dress with long sleeves and a low neckline.

Alex closes her eyes. "I'll never make up my mind. We should have asked Caroline to come."

"For what? So she can fuss about Edward or that awful night?"

Alex does not want to discuss that night, unsure of what she revealed without meaning to. She knows Penelope felt left out and wishes she could explain everything to her without saying a word about the beach and three years ago.

"Caroline won't be necessary, darling. I've decided on the black one. Now let's go buy stockings."

"I like this one," Alex says, holding the selected dress and knowing this makes no difference whatsoever to her friend.

Purchases in tow, they stop at the Clinique counter and examine the pale-green-and-silver products.

"This is a good color," Penelope says, holding up a pink lipstick.

"No. I absolutely draw the line here. Keeping the seams of my stockings straight is going to be hard enough, without having to worry about smeared lipstick and runny mascara."

"If you let me do your face, it won't smear. When you do it, it's a mess because you don't know how."

"Forget it, Penelope. Anyway, you can't make up my face; you have to get ready to see Colin."

"We're not going out until nine or so. He has rehearsal."

"You think you'll get him tonight?" Alex asks, following Penelope to the car.

"I have no idea. Time will tell."

They drive up Franklin Street. The sky is getting gray, and people are moving languidly in and out of stores and restaurants. Soon it will be Saturday night, and the street will be alive and full of people going to get drinks or ice cream or movie tickets. Now people are just getting ready, lazily making plans, knowing they will be out later in full force. Alex is glad to have a reason to go out. She feels connected to everyone else in town.

"Do you really think going out with him is a mistake?"

Penelope laughs. "Would I have gone to all this trouble if I thought you should stay at home?"

"Yes. You love to make me dress up." Boss me around.

"Caroline thinks I should let you make up your own mind."

"What good are friends if they don't tell you what to think?"

"I wish I could control Caroline's thinking," Penelope

says, pulling into Alex's driveway. "She's getting so mopey. It's a bore."

Alex remembers Penelope's golden rule: "You can step on my heart, be snotty, or rude, but never, never bore me." She told this to Alex when explaining how much she tried to break the rules of diplomacy. Alex had laughed then, picturing Penelope trying to put excitement into an embassy party, but now thinking of the rule scares her.

"Thanks for helping me," she says.

"Don't forget about your hair, darling."

The car drives off, and Alex walks slowly to her apartment, wondering if she is up for this. A cocktail party. She doesn't even drink.

"I need to go back to the house before dinner, Edward."

"Why?"

"Well, I need a sweater—"

"Wear one of mine."

If she didn't think it was rude, Susan would laugh. She's five feet five, Edward's six two. She drowns in his clothes.

"Also I need to make sure I haven't been scheduled for desk duty at the sorority."

"Oh, Christ."

"So, I'll meet you at Spanky's, okay?"

"Whatever."

"Are you mad?"

"No. I just never thought I'd see the day that a girl I knew, let alone dated, had 'desk duty.'"

She knows the girls he is thinking about are Alex and Penelope. Please God, not Caroline.

♦ ♦ ♦

Caroline watches her roommate Deena Jane get ready for her date. Caroline herself has spent the day in bed reading *Light in August*. Her paper on it is due Monday. The topic is "Christ Imagery in Faulkner." Alex just wrote a paper in comp. lit. entitled "Christ Imagery in Balzac." Caroline wonders if the faculty is in conspiracy with the Baptists. She is having trouble concentrating, and watching Deena Jane cover her mouth with lipstick and her pulse points with perfume is so fascinating. Of course even the ceiling is fascinating when you're supposed to be thinking about Christ imagery. Caroline thinks about calling Alex but remembers that tonight is the night Simon asked her out. She hopes Alex will have a good time, introduce herself as Alexandria, and not get uptight. She understands the uptightness now and wonders how Alex made it through all their late-night talks. She knows that if she listened to anyone even mention sex, her skin would burn where Bob had touched her, and her head aches from the effort of blocking his picture from her mind.

This is why she will not call Penelope.

"If he drives a silver Mazda, he's here," Cristen calls from the living room.

Alex has just gotten her stockings' seams straight, her breasts nicely arranged under the dress's neckline, and her hair up. Strands keep escaping from her barrette, but Cristen has assured her that this is sexy.

"He's really cute."

"Get away from that window," Alex says, coming out of her bedroom.

Cristen whistles. "Well, it was all worth it. Even your earrings look good."

Alex is wearing the five gold ones she wore to her father's club last Christmas. The doorbell rings. "I'll get it."

"I'll go to my room."

"My God," Simon says, "you're ready. This almost never happens to me. I was expecting to entertain your roommate for half an hour."

"Sorry," she says.

"No problem. I'll drive you around for a while. The twilight's very pretty."

"Let me get my coat," she says. She is really going to look in the mirror and check her hair.

She comes back out, and he helps her with her coat just the way her father does.

"You look very nice," he says.

If it were not for the look he gave her—the all-encompassing, head-to-toe devouring look—Alex would pack it in right now. By itself the word "nice" is equivalent to saying "interesting" when looking at bad modern art. But with that look, "nice" means "stunning, beautiful, lovely." With that look, "nice" means Alexandria.

He introduces her that way at the party. "This is Alexandria Rust. Alexandria, this is so and so."

She cannot keep any of the names straight. The party is in a large, drafty room with faded rugs and torn leather couches. Dark, heavy oil paintings of the fraternity's founding fathers hang on walls badly in need of a paint job. Men deposit their dates and then go get drinks and talk to the other "bros."

"This is normally the rec room," Simon tells her. "You should see it on football Saturdays."

"Oh, do you watch the game here?" she asks.

He looks at her blankly.

"You know, on television," she adds.

He steers her toward the bar. "No. We go to the game and then come back here and every fraternity on the court has a major blow-out. Haven't you ever come to one of the parties?"

She shakes her head.

He asks what she wants and then gets it for her.

"What do you do if we lose?" she asks.

The blank look again.

"You know, the game. Do you cancel the party?"

He laughs. "Alexandria, the game is just an excuse. Win or lose, it makes no difference—the DKE house will have a blow-out."

"Oh."

"Simon, man, where were you all day? I wanted to shoot pool." A boy with feathered brown hair and a blond date comes up to them.

"I was playing tennis with Fred."

"Did you kick his ass?"

"Yeah. I always kick his ass."

"Is that all you do to it?" Alex asks.

Simon's friend spills his drink. Simon laughs.

"Alexandria, this is my roommate, Robert Turnus."

She smiles. "You're the only person I've ever met with a more literary name than mine."

"The *Aeneid,*" Simon says to Robert. "You're named after the Durrell books?" he asks her.

"Yes."

Robert walks away. His girlfriend stays. Alex can count her ribs through her pink top. Around them men in khakis and white button-downs move about stationary women in brilliant pastels and floral prints. For once Penelope has made a mistake. Basic black just doesn't blend at the DKE house.

"I love all your earrings," says the girl in pink, "and your hair looks so distinguished that way."

Alex smiles. This girl sounds as breathy as Marilyn Monroe. Her face is well made up. "What's your name?"

"Ellen-Lynne Hope. I'm a Chi Omega. You must be a Kappa. I haven't ever seen you here before, and Robert's always going on how Simon likes the Kappas."

Alex looks at Simon. He is smiling at her with his eyes half-closed and his mouth tight, wanting to break into a laugh.

"I must be one, then," Alex says.

"Must be," Simon echoes.

"I knew it. I can always tell what house a girl comes from." Ellen-Lynne brushes some imaginary dust from her top. "My mother was a leg," she adds by way of explanation. "I should go find Robert. It was so nice to meet you, Alexandria. I hope Simon brings you by again."

Oh, yes. Me too. "Bye-bye," Alex says.

Simon puts his arm around her and steers her slowly across the room. "A Kappa," he says patiently, "is a member of the Kappa Kappa Gamma house. The girls in Chi O, generally about as swift as Ellen-Lynne, believe the Kappas to be an exotic bunch of girls, which really means they think the Kappas put out. A 'leg' is a legacy, which means that Ellen-Lynne's mother's mother was also in the Chi O sorority, which means it is a family tradition."

"I feel like an idiot," Alex says, wondering why Ellen-Lynne thinks she looks like a girl who puts out.

"That's okay. I feel like an interpreter," Simon says.

"You should take me to a football game," Alex says.

His voice sounds just the way Caroline's did that Saturday: kind, patient, and disbelieving. Funny that a man could sound like an Amazon.

"We'll have two cheeseburgers, a Michelob, and a Coke," Edward tells the waitress at Spanky's. "I'm glad you didn't have desk duty tonight."

Susan is not sure if he is making fun of her or not. She had decided to stop eating red meat after seeing this gross movie in anthropology about a tribe that ate cows raw. She forgot to tell Edward. Oh, well.

They stare at each other.

"I like your sweater," he says.

"Thank you."

"Are you still behind in your econ. class?"

She shrugs.

"How's work at the *Tar Heel*?"

"I quit."

"How come?"

"It was boring."

"Alex just loves it," he says, dragging out the "lex" of her name.

Of course, Alex writes things, interviews people, goes to movies. Alex does not move copy around in the backshop trying to make it fit on a page.

"I know," Susan says.

"You know."

"I know." She thinks it is a very good thing that they are going to a movie.

Penelope is looking at her phone and wishing she had some more wall space. Clearly, she is going to be alone tonight. Probably rehearsal has run late. Probably he has forgotten. She wishes now that she had waited for his call before tearing apart her closet and taking a bath. All dressed up and nowhere to go.

She reaches for the phone. She will call Alex. They'll go to a late show. No. Damn it. Alex is on a date. Caroline? No, that would be so obvious. It's not that she doesn't want to see Caroline, she just doesn't want to find out that all this time Caroline and Alex have been best friends, sharing things like rape and excluding her.

Maybe she'll go to sleep. Get up early. Call Alex for breakfast. Hear all the details. Penelope laughs. There are never any details with Alex.

"Poor darling," Penelope croons. "Poor, poor darling," she repeats until it occurs to her she is not sure who she means.

Alex is trying to talk to a boy who has approached her and said, "I'm in your class. Did you do that paper? On why the Christ imagery in Balzac is reversed?"

"It's the father in *Old Goriot* who is martyred, not a son, or in this case the daughters. You see?"

"No. You think he'll take a late paper?"

"I think Dr. Jordan is really sweet—" Alex begins, but is cut off.

"He is the biggest snot," the boy says. "He's always showing off. He talked about Norman Mailer for twenty minutes last class, and we're not even going to read him."

"That's not fair," Alex says. She turns to Simon. "Dr. Jordan was trying to explain why biography is irrelevant to literature. He said Mailer was a joke, but got read because of his life."

"Like Hemingway."

Alex smiles. "Yes, exactly."

The boy stares at them. "Simon," he says, "this girl is too smart for me. Get you a drink?"

"No."

Alex gnaws at one of her fingernails. She can hear Penelope saying, "Not in public, darling."

"I would like to see you defend me the way you did Dr. Jordan," Simon says.

"Do you speak ten languages?" Alex asks.

"Wouldn't do me much good if you didn't as well," Simon says. "However, if you did, that would make you too smart. Don't let Gerry bother you. He's a jerk."

She could like this man, and when he takes her home and leaves her at the door with a chaste and brotherly kiss, she decides that she does.

11

Tea Party

The backyard of Penelope's house reminds her of Center Court at Wimbledon on the last day, a lot of dust and a little grass struggling beneath moving feet. Penelope's favorite place as a child was the house in Vermont, where they went once a year and her father told all his brothers that England was "bloody super" or Paris was "amazingly lovely." The lawn went on forever, rolling into wild, unkempt woods. The lawn itself was not kept up very well. They were there so seldom that it hardly seemed worthwhile to keep everything lawn-tennis green, the way it was at the main house near London or later at the embassy in Paris. But there was, when she was still only four feet tall, a safeness in the Vermont gardens. No noisy sisters or enraged parents could find her if she chose to walk among the overgrown weeds.

At five feet eleven, she still longs for the Vermont home the way Caroline recalls Carl: the memory grows richer and sweeter than the reality, as the years pass.

Looking at the dustiness of the Carr Street yard makes Penelope want to cry. Instead she places a tray with teacups and small square biscuits on a low metal table and goes inside to put the water on. It is Penelope's desire to share her home life with her friends without ever actually bringing them to England, where her mother insisted on keeping the house after her father's appointment. Every Friday at four Penelope has an open-house tea, and though sometimes only Alex and Caroline show up, frequently a lot of hungry Bullfoots appear to check up on each other. ("And what committees are you on?" "Did you hear he might run for Student Body president? The foundation would like that." "I think she's bucking for the Rhodes. She doesn't have a chance.") Today is also Alex's twentieth birthday, and Penelope thinks it will be nice for Alex to have a little party. A big one would be out of place. She will throw Alex a huge party next year for her twenty-first.

Penelope smiles and pours the cloudy water into a chipped enamel yellow pot. She knows that someone today will be sure to whisper, "Did you know, poor Penelope has hooked up with a gay man. When will she get serious?" Outside, Alex is sitting on one of the low garden chairs slopping jam on a biscuit and pushing her shoes out of sight. She says hi to Penelope and then says with disgust, "You invited Kate Poser?"

"I've missed three classes of the African seminar, and Kate takes copious notes."

"Well, then don't fuss at me. I asked Simon to come around."

"Oh, Alex, really. Well, it's your day. Hello, Kate, what an interesting hat."

It is Alex's conviction that Kate suffers from a severe Zelda Fitzgerald complex, and Kate's blousy dresses and hats amuse Penelope greatly. Alex looks at the pink monstrosity on Kate's head and, avoiding Penelope's steely composure, gags down some tea.

Colin arrives with three red carnations, which he presents to Penelope with a little bow.

"Hello, beautiful," he says, and while Penelope is glad he says it within earshot of Kate, she wants to scream at him, "Tell me, Colin, is different still a good thing?" She looks forward to the day when she will not speak to men who allow play rehearsals to keep her waiting.

She hands Edward a cup of tea. He is quizzing Alex on the whereabouts of Simon.

"I told him to come, Edward. Now back off."

"Alex, you should have brought him. He'll never come alone."

"Why not?"

"He'd be afraid."

"Edward, contrary to popular Bullfoot opinion, not all southerners are the nitwits that Susan is."

"Alex, she's not all that bad."

"I know, Edward, she is lovely to look at."

He fidgets with one of her earrings. "Alex, sometimes I don't know if I should kiss you or slap you right across the mouth."

Alex finishes swallowing her tea. "You condescending

bastard," she says. "The day you put a hand on me you better hope it's to slap me. You'll get off easier. Furthermore—"

Edward is saved by Penelope, who, having heard all of this, takes Edward's arm, moves him away, and asks:

"Did you invite her?"

"No, Penelope, I didn't, and I am getting tired of being treated badly by my best friends because of the woman I am sleeping with."

Show-off, Penelope thinks. "I don't care who you fuck, Edward, I'm just not up to another emotional upheaval on Caroline's part."

"What's this? Discord among the Amazons?"

"Not exactly. Let's just say there are strains."

"You all still heading for the mountains for fall break?"

"No, Alex finked out on us. She's going to Jonesfeld." Penelope does not add that she is extremely relieved.

"So what are you going to do?"

"I'm going home with Terry Kapel, remember her? My roommate freshman year."

"Edward, come say hi to Simon," Alex calls. She has decided to forgive Edward and speak to him, if only to keep Simon from running his hand across her neck.

"Hey, Reels, how you doing?"

"Great. Missed you in philosophy this morning."

Edward winks over Alex's head and says, "I slept in."

Simon, who has not been sleeping in with Alex, winks back and moves off to say hi to Colin, whose lover was in Simon's fraternity.

"Like him?" Edward asks, crouching down to whisper.

"Much more to the point, sweet Edward, is does he like me?"

"Yes, I expect so. Guys don't usually ask you out if they don't like you."

Alex laughs. "I haven't always found this to be true."

"Is he 'cute'? I've never been able to figure out what you girls consider passable."

"Yes, he's cute, just not knock-me-out cute, so Penelope will be rude."

Edward and Alex look over to where Simon and Colin are talking. Edward sees Penelope work her way over to the two men and tell them that there's beer inside. She puts her arm around Colin's neck and smiles at Simon sweetly.

"No, she won't, look."

Alex laughs and kisses Edward on the cheek. When she reaches for her tea, she sees Caroline and starts to wave her over, but Caroline turns abruptly around and walks down the driveway to the street.

Well, fuck her, Alex thinks. I'm getting tired of this. Edward's a dear, but no one is worth this amount of trauma. I'll bet she even forgot today is my birthday. I'd never forget hers.

"Do you really think Susan's lovely?" Edward asks suddenly.

"Absolutely. I'd like to be just like her." Alex shakes her hair out and goes off to claim Simon.

"Having fun?" she asks softly into his ear.

"Loads." He puts his arm around her waist and says, after looking carefully around, "I think you should tell Penelope that Colin likes boys."

Alex laughs. "She knows. That's what makes him so very attractive."

"Oh."

"Yes, oh."

"Who's that?" Simon asks, pointing to a small girl who is sitting at the foot of a tree surrounded by six of Simon's frat brothers and looking a lot like Scarlett O'Hara at the Wilkeses' barbecue.

"That's Susu Sleaney. She's adorable. People are always falling in love with her. She's a great fan of Penelope's."

Susu Sleaney always introduces herself by following her name with "I'm from Alabama," as if to explain the Susu. Caroline used to ask who in the world would inflict the name "Susu" on a child. Susu, who once dated a homosexual for six months thinking his biggest defect was that he was Jewish, follows Penelope's doomed love affairs with great relish and comes to tea as often as she can.

"Is everyone here a 'great fan of Penelope's'?" Simon asks.

"No, not quite. See him?" Alex points to a very tall boy with a prominent Adam's apple. "That's Kevin Holley. He once asked her out, and she just cut him dead. I don't know why. He's really dear."

Kevin tried to teach her pool in the basement of the Student Union. She was wearing a scooped-neck T-shirt and no bra. He stood at one end of the table, directing her shot, and suddenly turned red and moved away. Alex was amused and touched. The James Harringtons of the world would have stayed. Alex has always been sorry that Kevin, having struck out with one Amazon, will never try another.

"Listen, shall I take you to dinner tonight, seeing how it's your birthday?"

"Oh," Alex says with glee and disappointment, "that's so nice, but I've got to get some work done tonight. I'm two novels behind in my English class, and with fall break coming up, I have to get my ass in gear."

"Well, what if you study until eleven or so and then we go out?"

"Great. That would be wonderful."

"You want to go see *Annie Hall*? It's the late show."

"I never," Alex says slowly and deliberately, "want to see another Woody Allen film again."

"I thought you liked him."

"Past tense."

"Okay, I'll think of something better. Look, I better see if Edward needs notes from this morning."

Alex laughs. "No way," she says. "This place is a regular note brokerage."

"I'll be right back." Simon wanders to the garden's edge, where Edward is considering the crowd.

Alex pours herself a cup of tea and puts jam on another muffin. Edward and Simon keep glancing her way. Edward is probably telling Simon how smart she is. Now they are looking at her legs. In fact, they are both looking at her in the way Alex expects men to look at Susan. What is the deal? They cannot be saying she is beautiful, certainly not cute. If she had one of them in a class, she would expect requests for notes. Simon makes a vague gesture with his hands, and Edward nods in agreement. They look at her again. She will have to ask Edward.

"Has Caroline come?" Penelope has momentarily left Colin.

"No—I mean yes, she came, saw me buss Edward, and disappeared."

"What a rotter."

"No, she's just unhappy."

"Exactly. Excuse me, darling, I have got to get hold of Kate before she leaves."

"Alex..." Edward approaches her. "I'm going. Have a good time—"

"Alexandria," Simon interrupts, "how about *The Wall*? You want to see that?"

"Sure."

"I'll pick you up," Simon says to her. "Bye," he says to Edward.

"Hold on, Reels, I'll walk with you." Simon waits halfway down the driveway.

"Anyway, enjoy Jonesfeld," Edward says.

"Thanks. Are you and Susan staying here or going to New York?"

Edward smiles. "I'm going to Manhattan, and she's going to Greensboro to see her mom."

"I thought she lived in Raleigh."

"Her dad does. It's weird. She's very uptight about going to see her mom."

"Maybe she was an abused child, which explains why she always whispers."

"Good-bye, Alex."

"Just kidding, Edward. She's not that bad. She thinks I'm pretty."

"Yeah, she told me. Just what I need. My girl and my best friend hooking up."

"Don't be disgusting," Alex says. "She is not *your* girl."

"All right. I've got to go."

"Edward, what were you and Simon talking about?"

"You."

"What did you say?" she asks with an even mixture of interest and anxiety.

"Sorry. Guy talk. You know how it is."

She watches him saunter down the driveway to meet Simon and knows that he has just taken his revenge for the countless "girl talks" she, Penelope, and Caroline have inflicted on him. Damn. She sees Kate Poser and Penelope part. Penelope bounds up to Alex's side.

"Marvelous, I got Kate's notes and Colin came."

Alex picks up the tea tray. "I'm glad, Penelope, I really am."

Penelope puts her hand on Alex's arm. "Leave those," she says. "I want to go on the roof."

Weather permitting, they use Penelope's roof like a beach. They crank up Penelope's stereo, climb out through the window, and fry.

"I don't have my suit," Alex says. "And anyway it's past four."

"I don't want the sun, I just want to feel super-big."

Alex laughs. "Okay."

"What do you want to hear?" Penelope asks as she opens her bedroom window.

"Do you still have my Helen Reddy album?"

"Yeah, I'll put it on."

Alex stands against the chimney listening to Reddy's husky voice boom, "If I have to/I can do anything/I am Woman."

"It must be nice to feel that way," Penelope says, lying dangerously close to the drainpipe.

"Don't you ever?" "I am strong, I am invincible" is just how Alex feels after a thorough purge.

"Oh, sure, just not twenty-four hours."

"Nobody does."

"A lot of people, darling, think that we do."

Alex sits down, crumpling some dead leaves in her hand. "They're just confusing being tough with having confidence."

"Oh, look..." Penelope points up to the sky. This is

one of those rare afternoons when the moon is already visible, looking like a pop-out cloud.

"Pretty," Alex says disinterestedly. "Jack Paterson told Simon I was a virago."

"You can't possibly listen to anything Jack Paterson ever says."

Jack is the president of Simon's fraternity. He was not at the party Simon took her to: he just heard about Alex from the "brothers." He is famous on campus for talking women into bed; he cannot charm them, stare them, or attract them there, so he talks them. Nobody is sure what he says, but everyone is sure that it works.

"What does it mean, anyway?" Penelope looks at Alex's blank face. "Virago," she says.

"Oh. Well, Simon says the word is used as bitch, but when he looked it up it meant female warrior."

"For Christ's sake, it's just another word for Amazon."

"Yeah, but I don't want Simon's fraternity brothers running around calling me a female warrior."

Penelope inches in a little from the roof's edge. "When I was twelve my parents took us to Greece, and before we got to Athens Daddy gave us each a copy of Robert Graves's myths. I just fell in love with Artemis."

"Really? Wasn't she the one who turned a man into a stag just for looking at her naked?" Alex asks in a teasing voice.

"Yes. His dogs devoured him," Penelope says with relish. "But she was so pure and strong. Goddess of the hunt, chastity, and the moon. I loved her and thought that she followed me around everywhere, protecting my virtue. The perfect female warrior. Imagine my disgust when I found I liked men. All my sisters wanted to be Aphrodite."

"Funny, I wanted to be Athena," Alex says. "I thought I could be smarter than she was and prevent the whole Trojan war. 'Paris,' I would have said, 'pick me. With wisdom you can achieve all the wealth you want and win great battles, and having done both, no woman will resist you.' I thought I could have saved a lot of people a lot of grief."

"And, darling, deprived the world of some great stories. I stayed up all night finishing the *Iliad.* There was something about Achilles fighting a river out of grief for his dead friend. There was something so noble and mysterious and, well, pure about him and Patroclus. It was like finding Artemis all over again."

Alex crumbles some leaves over Penelope's face. "You're pretty dumb, Miz Samms. They were fucking each other. That's why Achilles was so pissed off at Hector for killing him."

Penelope sits up, shaking her head. "I know that, Alex. But they were men and they loved each other and it was beautiful." Penelope pauses. "I've been thinking about switching to classics."

"Classics what?"

"For my major. I hate our novel course."

"That's because you hate Virginia Woolf."

"True."

"The only one I've finished yet is *A Room of One's Own.*"

"That's something I'll never have to worry about."

"What is?"

"Having a room and an income. I have a trust fund waiting for me to have a baby or turn thirty. It's something I remember every time I turn on a vacuum."

"I know. You make me sick."

"Oh, Alex, there'd always be a place for you in my room."

"Did I hear you say he was a-meeting you here today/ To take you to his castle in the sky," Reddy sings out.

For a minute the contrast of Penelope's pale lashes against her dark skin keeps Alex mesmerized. "Do you know," she says slowly, "I believe you mean that."

"Of course I do, darling. You're my favorite Amazon."

Alex thinks of Caroline's stiff, angry retreating back. I'm your only Amazon, she thinks.

"Good," she says. "Good."

12.

Fall Break

When Alex gets off Eastern's flight 56 into Boston, she is carrying an overnight bag and a red rose with brown edges. Simon sent it over to her apartment that morning. Cristen had opened the door in her long red bathrobe.

"Yeah?"

A nervous pledge from Simon's fraternity asked, "Does Alexandria Rust live here?"

"Yes, yes, she does. Alex!!"

Alex came out of her room in a T-shirt. She does not own a robe. "What is it?"

"This is for you," the boy said, thrust a long thin package into her arms, and disappeared. While Alex took the rose out of its wax paper, Cristen opened the card that had fallen to the ground.

"I'm not completely tactless, love Simon," she read. "What the hell does that mean?"

"Give me that!" She went to the kitchen and ran water in a wineglass.

"Put on your Billy Joel, would you, Cristen?"

The night before, when Alex had said, "No, I don't think so," to Simon's suggestion that they make love, he'd said, "Alexandria," very slowly as if he were tasting her name. "How odd that you have no romance in your soul. How odd when the books you're named for deal exclusively and relentlessly with love."

"Yeah? Well, you have no tact, which I suppose isn't so odd." Then she'd disappeared into her apartment, slamming the door.

Now, making her way through Logan, she is glad that she brought the flower with her. It reminds her that she has a reason to go back to Chapel Hill, ties to the place outside of Penelope and Caroline. She forgets this sometimes. On line at the taxi stand a young man in a blue suit and yellow tie asks if she is going into Boston.

"No. Jonesfeld."

"Too bad. We could have . . . shared a cab."

She looks at him. He's handsome in a yuppie sort of way. "Yeah, too bad." She brings the rose to her nose and smiles. She has always wanted to do that, smile at a man across flowers, telling him, with a touch of sorrow, that she is unavailable.

When she tells the cab driver she is going to Jonesfeld,

his whole face lights up. It should. The ride will cost her twenty-five dollars. The blue-black night rushes by with silver streaks that Alex knows are stars.

When the car turns into the campus, Alex looks at the big Gothic buildings scattered among velvet lawns and says, "Oh, my God, this place does look like a nunnery."

The taxi driver turns around and gives her a smile. "Well, it does have a nunnery's basic requirements."

Alex laughs and rolls down her window. "Hey," she calls to a passing girl in a big fur coat. "Where is Kaila dorm?"

The fur coat approaches and gives the driver instructions.

"Funny thing," he says, making a U-turn, "you sure didn't look like a Jonesfeld girl, but I figured you had to be."

Alex decides to take this as a compliment but, because you can never be sure, does not overtip.

In the lobby Alex goes to the front desk.

"Celia Douglass," says the girl into the intercom, "you have a visitor."

Alex grimaces. Despite the calendar hanging on the wall behind the desk, the 1980s have yet to visit Jonesfeld, where "visitors" are women and "callers" are men.

Two hands cover Alex's eyes. She turns around and gives Celia a big hug.

"It's good to see you."

"How was your flight?"

Alex shrugs. "How is any flight?" She follows Celia up some stairs to the room. "Where's your roommate?" she asks, looking at the bright yellow room with two big beds that look more like overstuffed couches. Thinking of the cell she and Caroline had to share last year, Alex shudders and realizes that this is one of the places where tuition differences show up.

"I told her to take off for the weekend."

"Great, I'd been prepping myself to enjoy sleeping on the floor, and—"

Celia laughs. "Oh, Alex, I'd never let you sleep on the floor. It wouldn't be pretty."

Alex gives her another hug. Celia rummages through her desk. "Want some coke?"

"No, but I'll take a Tab."

"Not that kind, silly." From a drawer Celia removes a brown envelope and a silver spoon. "This."

"Since when do you do coke?"

"Since...I don't know. This term. I was so tired.... Does it matter?"

"No, I'm just surprised."

Celia bends down over her desk. When she looks up she reminds Alex of a pale white cartoon character colored with a red crayon.

"So, what are we going to do?"

"Go to a few classes, show you around, maybe go to Cambridge. Whatever."

"Whatever," Alex echoes, remembering the visits she made to the Douglass country house in New Hampshire, where Celia would post a schedule on the wall: 7:00 wake up; 7:30 walk to market; 8:00 breakfast; 9:00 go to club and swim; 12:00 lunch; and so on. Even free time was on the list (4:00 to 5:00 before setting the table). How strange that Celia should abandon the one family habit that would have made college life easier. Alex can remember endless treks up and down 57th Street while

Celia scouted out good gallery locations. "I don't want to be a downtown dealer," she would say.

Alex wonders what Celia wants to be now.

Before going to sleep, Alex realizes that this was the first time she ever saw anyone do coke. Which is pretty damn funny in light of the fact that her first few days at college she was forever fielding questions like "Do you go to the Palladium? Have you been mugged? You can *walk* in Central Park? Do you deal?"

The next morning, while Celia goes to class, Alex jogs through the campus trying to do her five-mile Chapel Hill run at Jonesfeld. It's very distracting here. There are real lawns scattered across campus with green velvet grass and neat flower beds. There are stone castlelike buildings everywhere. The women she passes are almost all the kind you could have a field day with playing scrutiny. She and Penelope are lucky to see three interesting candidates in an hour.

At ten she meets Celia at the cafeteria. There are big red plastic tables with matching chairs. Girls in tight black jeans, leather jackets, and short hair sit smoking and eating yogurt and talking in deep Marlene Dietrich voices. Girls in Peter Pan collars, pink sweaters, and plaid skirts sit, going over notebooks and sipping orange juice. Alex buys a yogurt and a granola bar and then surveys the place while waiting for Celia. She is really trying to figure out where her friend fits into this tightly segregated scene. Maybe that's why Celia bagged art history, a life-long passion. There doesn't seem to be a place here for too much individuality. Maybe Celia is just looking for her place amid the stereotypes. Alex cannot really picture her with Caroline or Penelope, whose counterparts may or may not be at Jonesfeld. She picks a table near one, where a girl with blond hair and a face full of planes and angles sits ignoring her three tablemates. Watching the girl smoke makes Alex wonder if maybe she shouldn't pick up the habit.

Celia joins her with a plate full of eggs. Alex makes a face. Eggs are impossible to throw up.

"Well, what do you think?" Celia queries.

Alex has just seen a young man come in—a professor?—followed by three plaid skirts—students? "For the first time in my life," she says, "I feel an identification with a man. He looks like an exotic plant, and I feel like one."

Celia laughs. "Men are pretty rare here. But it's good. All the buildings are named after women, and our newspaper writes about women's issues all the time. We'd never advocate replacing Helen Reddy's 'I Am Woman' with 'Material Girl.'"

"I'd forgotten that I'd written you about that."

"You were explaining Penelope to me—that she'd never heard of Helen Reddy."

"Oh. What else did I say? Anything that would make you want to meet her?"

"Not terribly." Celia pushes eggs around the plate. "I'm not sure I like women so much."

Alex sticks her yogurt lid into the empty container. "Gee, thanks."

"Alex, I don't think of you as a woman."

"I've heard that one before," she says, thinking of countless study lunches with nervous men, her dateless evenings, of the people who walk away from her murmuring, "Too smart."

"I think of you as my friend. I can't really imagine

being friends with the women here. They're so, so..."

"Fake," Alex supplies, thinking of the fur coat giving directions, the blond smoking.

"Yeah. You can't imagine anyone here having trouble deciding what to do with their lives. They'll either marry someone from Harvard or set up radical lesbian communes. Not planning on doing either of those, I don't really fit in."

Fit in. Alex studies Celia's sweet freckled face, remembers staying up late with her to watch old movies and manicure their nails. How well they fit into each other's lives then. She is about to say, "Only Susan fits in," but realizes that Celia has no idea who Susan is.

"You want to go into Cambridge later?" she says instead.

"Sure."

On the bus to Harvard, Celia tells Alex she has been seeing a counselor at Mental Health.

"How come?"

Celia looks out the window. "I told you that I dropped Art fifty, right?"

"Yes."

"Well, I just feel at sea."

"At sea how?" Alex never feels anchored. She's always assumed that's normal.

"I called my parents and told them I was dropping art and would therefore have to change my major, right? Well, my dad just got off the phone, and my mom said, 'That's nice, dear,' and hung up."

Alex laughs. Last year she dropped astronomy—it was at 8:00 A.M., and she kept sleeping through it. Two weeks later she received two thick letters—one from each parent. "When I was at Columbia I took eight courses, including Latin and Greek. You are not there to fritter your time away, no matter how 'relaxed' everyone down south is. . . ." wrote her father. "You need a science to graduate, Alexandria. This is your life you're playing with, get it together!" wrote her mother. Alex had thought about her 3.6 GPA and wondered if anything in the world was ever enough.

Right now she's having trouble seeing Celia's problem. But she realizes from looking at Celia's face that she should not have laughed. Maybe Celia is more than at sea, maybe she is in a tidal wave.

"Is that when you started doing coke?" she asks in a low voice.

Celia looks annoyed. "For God's sake, Alex. What's the difference?"

"Nothing."

In Cambridge they argue over where to eat, and over dinner they argue about where a better social life can be found—single-sex or coed campuses.

"It's not like you're batting a thousand down there," Celia snaps.

"That's true. But there I can meet guys naturally. Relationships aren't based solely on sex."

"Bullshit. Why do you keep getting dumped? I'll tell you: sex."

Alex is surprised to hear Celia being so on target. Still, she's a little offended. "At least I get dumped. When's the last time you were on a date?" With horror she sees Celia blink hard over eyes that are filling. "Oh, Celia, it's not important. You're happy, and that's important." And not quite true, Alex thinks. She has become so accustomed to Penelope's and Caroline's imperviousness that she has forgotten how to talk to people. Perhaps the Amazon

Club, the scrutiny game, life in general, is making her hard.

"Celia, men are a drag. I think it would be easier to go to school here."

"Nothing," Celia says, savagely spearing a tortellini shell, "is easy about going to school here."

What to say, what to say? Wouldn't transferring be an admission of failure? Alex looks at Celia, and the unhappiness confronting her is too much.

"Let's get dessert," Alex says. It rings false and ugly. Alex never eats dessert, and she can tell from the way her friend is looking at her that Celia knows this.

That night they go to the Jonesfeld Student Union, where *Ordinary People* is playing. Alex cries all the way through it, but Celia just says shortly, "Timothy Hutton's cute, but what a dumb fuck, couldn't even do that right."

Alex, embarrassed about her red eyes, pushes her hair into her face. "Do what right?"

"Kill himself. I mean, how hard can it be?"

"I would guess very."

"Not if you really want to."

Alex wonders when it was that they had become so different. She wonders if she knew when, if she could correct the split. She thinks about Penelope and Caroline and realizes that splits are splits, not terribly mendable.

In the car, on the way to Terry's house, Penelope tries to convince herself that going to Fayetteville will be fun. She has never seen an army base before, and Terry's father is a sergeant.

"My grandmother will be there," Terry is saying, "so be prepared to eat a lot."

"Okay." Penelope wonders where Colin is going this

weekend. She has not spoken to him since her tea party. "Welcome to Fayetteville," says a green sign on the freeway.

"The whole town caters to the base," Terry says. "That makes it nice to be an army brat. There are some places like, ugh, Texas, where everyone just hates you if you live on base." At the gate Terry's father is waiting with their passes, which will let them come and go hassle free from overzealous guards.

"How are you, babe?" he asks Terry, giving her a kiss and then climbing in the backseat.

"Just great, Daddy. This is Penelope Samms."

Penelope offers her hand and says, "How do you do, sir?" in her clippest of tones.

Sergeant Kapel stares at her a minute. He has not been forewarned. "You got an accent?" he asks.

"Penelope's from Paris, Daddy."

"Illinois?" Sergeant Kapel had not been part of D-Day.

"No," Penelope says. She wishes Alex could see this scene.

"She's from France, Daddy. Her father works there."

Penelope smiles. You could call it work; no one else would.

"Well, how 'bout that. You like the States?"

"Oh, yes. I'm really American, because of my parents. But I was raised in England."

She has thoroughly confused him, but now they've arrived at the Kapel house.

"Honey, I've got to get back to the barracks. Good recruits this year, but there's always the bad seed. Go in an' see your ma."

They carry their stuff inside, and a small carrot-topped girl comes out of the kitchen. "Terry!"

"Hello, Selina. Say hi to Penelope. Penelope, this is Selina, my sister."

"Hello."

Selina will not answer. She's turned coy.

"Where's Peter?" Terry asks.

"He's not here anymore."

"What do you mean?" Terry puts her sister down and takes Penelope into the kitchen.

"He and Daddy had a monster fight, and Peter got sent away."

"Another fight? What about?"

" 'Bout Mommy."

"Again?"

"Yup. Daddy hit her, Peter yelled, and the next morning he went to Camp Lejeune. He said I'd been there, but I don't remember. Was I?"

"Yes," Terry says slowly. "We lived there for six months before you were two. Is that why Grandma's here?"

"I guess. Mommy has a broken leg."

Penelope wonders if Sergeant Kapel broke it. She's amazed at Terry's calm. Good manners cannot cover a chatterbox sister's news.

Terry suddenly looks at her guest. "Sorry about this. No one in the family writes except Peter, and I just didn't realize Dad would ever pull rank to get him transferred."

"Peter's a soldier?"

"Oh, yeah. The whole damn family. Your dad passes on money, mine a career. Poor Peter never even wanted it." Terry shakes her head. "Oh, well. I'd better go see my mom. Selina, get Penelope a Coke."

"Okay." Selina slid off her seat. "Warm or cold?"

"Cold, please."

"It's easier to burp with warm, but okay. You're probably too pretty to be gross."

Penelope opens the proffered can. "Is burping gross?"

"You bet. That's what Peter says. Daddy does it with beer, but still."

"Listen," Penelope says, and delivers a small burp, gurgling up from the base of her throat. Penelope has three brothers and five sisters. She is the baby, and one summer, in the house in Vermont, they devoted themselves to teaching her how to burp and then convinced her to show their father. She got all her candy money taken away because she showed him at the dinner table when company was over.

Selina is impressed with Penelope's effort. "Peter says that's not ladylike."

"I'm not a lady," returns Penelope, relishing the phrase. "I'm not a lady," she told her father when he admonished her for turning cartwheels in the hall.

"That's not how a lady behaves, Penelope Anne."

"I'm not a lady."

"Oh, yes, you are. You're mine, ergo you're a lady. I raise ladies."

"Perhaps," Penelope said slowly, "I'm a bastard." She was repeating a word heard on the playground, and she knew it was terrible because the girl who had no father who'd been called that cried all afternoon and had to be sent home.

Her father slapped her, but she was satisfied—being ninth meant you had to try harder, take chances. Gamble and win. "Gamble and win," Penelope repeats.

"What?" asks Selina.

"Nothing." Penelope takes the girl in her lap, and an old woman with thick black hair comes in.

"Hello, I'm Terry's grandmother."

"Hello. Pleased to meet you, Mrs. Kapel."

The old woman laughs. "God forbid," she says. "The name's Leanest. God forbid I should be that son-of-a-bitch's mother."

"Oh, I'm, I'm terribly sorry."

"No problem. Go and make yourself at home while Terry talks to her mother."

"Okay."

Selina takes Penelope into the den to show her Sergeant Kapel's guns and television.

Mrs. Kapel presides silently over dinner with a swollen face and plaster-encased leg. During dinner, which is indeed huge, Selina whispers continuously into Penelope's ear.

"Eat those, they're slimy but good," she says, pointing to the okra on Penelope's plate. "They're better fried, but we have to watch Daddy's blood pressure. It always goes up after he knocks Mom around."

Penelope cannot believe this. Everyone is ignoring Selina; in fact, everyone is ignoring everyone. They are just eating—cornbread, ham with pineapple, peas, tomatoes, okra, baked potatos, and grits with cheese. Penelope thinks she is going to die, contemplates throwing up, remembers Alex, changes her mind.

"Peter loves cornbread," Selina whispers as Penelope reaches for some. "Grandma must be pretending he's not gone. She made the grits for Terry. She doesn't make anything for Daddy because she's so mad at him."

Still no one says anything. Sergeant Kapel takes a long swallow of beer and puts some more ham on his plate.

Penelope's father carves things into paper-thin slices,

pours wine, asks about their day, and then proceeds not to listen. She has seen him ignore knock-down-drag-out fights between her sisters over everything from a borrowed hair ribbon to a stolen boyfriend. She has seen him lecture on the Nazi blitzkrieg when one of them had a modern European history test. She has seen him get purple in the face over her using "fuck" at the dinner table. She has never seen anything like this.

"Pass the peas," Selina whispers. "Grandma made those for *me.*"

After the dishes have been done and Sergeant Kapel has settled in front of the TV and Selina has been put to bed, Terry takes Penelope on a tour. The base is all paved road with ugly green buildings rising up from the asphalt.

"That's the infirmary, that's the mess hall, supply house, Dad's barracks, Peter's..." Terry is pointing all over, and each new building looks like the last. Penelope realizes she'd better not get lost by going out on her own.

"Where did Peter live?" she asks, trying to orient herself and dying to know more about this boy who tries to protect his mother. It seems very exciting, if a little vulgar.

"With us. I can't believe Dad sent him away."

"Why not? That's what fathers are for. I went to eleven boarding schools in England. My father wasn't up to another round of that, so here I am. Shipped off to the States that he kept telling me were really home anyway."

"I remember the first time I heard you say that, that America was just a place you'd gone to for vacations. I wasn't sure I'd make it through the year with you."

The feeling, Penelope thinks, was totally mutual. Terry came to school equipped with a stereo, refrigerator, TV, and matching bedspreads. Penelope sat on her steamer trunk (a relic from her mother's youth) and watched the stuff pour in. The university hires people to help freshmen move into the dorms, knowing chaos will occur otherwise. When Terry finally appeared—a chunky, brown-haired, pleasant-faced girl—Penelope was so bewildered she could only stammer out a very crisp "How do you do?" It had been rough. Terry cooked in the room and wasn't very neat, but they'd gone out together a few dateless Saturday nights and surprised each other.

"Anyway, I always thought it was the scholarship that bribed you here."

Penelope laughs. "Terry, although the Bullfoot is a highly coveted prize in North Carolina, it doesn't mean shit in England—or Paris, for that matter. I was most definitely sent here through the wishes of me dad."

"Well, you see, 'me dad' is not even Peter's father."

"Who isn't?" The echoing "me dad" has confused her.

"My father. The great Sergeant Kapel."

"Really? I didn't realize your mother was married before."

"She wasn't. The quarterback at her high school got her 'into trouble,' as they say, and my dad saved her ass."

"Does Peter know?"

"Oh, yeah. They both do. And they hate each other. It's too ridiculous for words. Daddy figures Mom owes him something, that he's, you know, within his rights to hit her. And Peter doesn't see it that way."

"Do you?"

Terry shrugs. "I think it's funny that my mother got pregnant before getting married. She must have loved whoever it was, and I'm sorry that guy didn't marry her. You wouldn't know this, but that's a pretty big scandal in the South." She says this so matter-of-factly that Penelope is sure Terry means it, but wonders how she can.

"Funny?"

"Sure. My mother is a fallen woman, and everyone acts like no one is supposed to know. It's supposed to be this enormous secret."

She wonders why Terry has chosen to tell her something so private.

"It's nice you can be so casual about it," she says.

"Well, I've almost always known about it. It's easy to tell you, because you don't really know me well enough to pass a valid judgment."

Well, that makes sense, and she suddenly understands why Alex kept her rape a secret. If something upsets you, you don't want to share the humiliation and pain with a friend. Last year Penelope had told Terry about her own mother's affair with her father's secretary, but she's never revealed this vulnerability to Alex, whose skill at scrutiny terrifies her. Alex could do a lot with that information if her love ever drifts off, as Caroline's seems to.

"People make judgments all the time," Penelope bursts out. "Just sitting in the Pit, I judge people by how they look and who they're with."

Very carefully, Terry says, "I said valid judgments, Penelope. A lot of the people I've seen you dismiss are actually quite decent, and you would see that if you had valid criteria."

Penelope feels as if she has been slapped. She remembers overhearing Alex tell Edward, "I'm suffering from the Penelope complex. I either love someone all the way, or I can't be bothered by them." At the time she'd been amused by Alex summing her up so perfectly, but now she thinks there's nothing perfect about that kind of behavior.

She's a bit angry at getting a lecture from someone as different from her as Terry, but Terry's actually a decent person, or so she's always thought. She remembers Terry's placid face as she digested the news of her mother's leg and decides that the lecture may be justified.

Is this America? she wonders. Did her father leave to spare her this? She doesn't really belong here, but she hates Paris, too. England. Her mind latches on to England. It is home and focused. In England no one pretended her father was anything but a fancy vacuum salesman. None of that ambassador junk. In England people understood her and did not correct her grammar. In England the family had friends, not political connections. She longs for it with the fierceness that she used to have in her love for Alex and Caroline. And it surprises her to realize that the intensity of love is ebbing, surprises and scares her.

She studies Terry's face, pictures her growing up in places like this all her life. Penelope knows she could not subsist on Terry's company alone. She is addicted to Amazons; whatever criteria she holds up, they meet.

"Come this way," Terry says. "That's where the higher officers live, that's the rec hall, that the base school, that's where they keep the tanks, and that's it. All clear?"

"Absolutely."

Susan parks her car across the road from 240 Spring Street. What is she doing here? She hasn't seen her mother since her last birthday, has never stayed with her, and she has never seen her mother's lover, Lavinia. So Susan just sits in the car chewing on her add-a-beads. Finally, she picks up her suitcase and gets out of the car. She slams the door, silencing the whining sound it makes. She smooths out her cords and walks across the street. Immediately the door opens. It is her mother, tall, erect, bony, like all the pictures of her that Susan kept in a shoebox under her bed after the divorce.

"Oh, thank God," Mrs. Simmons says. "I was watching from the window, and I thought you were going to drive away."

Susan puts her suitcase down and crosses her arms across her chest. "I almost did," she says.

"It's okay. What matters is you didn't. Come in."

Her mother takes her suitcase, and Susan follows, thinking, So this is what it's like to walk behind your mother. To recognize your legs and ass on an older woman. I've always wondered.

"I've put you in the front downstairs room. It's where Lavinia's son always stays, and it has its own bathroom."

"Lavinia has a son?" Susan asks, sitting down gingerly on the edge of the bed.

"Three, actually, but two of them don't speak to her."

I got to meet these guys, Susan thinks. "Oh," she says.

"You're very pretty," her mother tells her.

"Thank you. I have a boyfriend."

Mrs. Simmons laughs. "I would expect so. Several, I hope."

"Just one. It's enough." Why did I say that? What am I doing here?

"Lavinia's at work now. I took the day off—I felt sick this morning."

"Me too."

"Do you want anything?"

"Mom?" There, now it's said.

"Yes?"

"Why, why . . . ?" She can't finish.

"Susan, I can't answer those questions. Not any more than I can tell you the meaning of life."

"I'd like a Coke."

"Will Tab do? We don't eat sugar."

"Tab's fine." Susan looks around after her mother goes out. There is a Cheryl Tiegs poster on the wall and a Christie Brinkley calendar on the wall turned to August. Either that's Lavinia's son's favorite picture, or he hasn't been here in a while. Or else her mother and Lavinia put it there. No. Surely they are too old for that sort of thing.

She goes out into the kitchen. Her mother is running water over a tray of ice.

"Would you like to go out or stay in tonight?"

The last thing Susan wants to do is go out in public with two dykes, but she just says, "Whatever is easiest for you. I don't care."

Her mother hands her a Tab. "Why don't we just stay in?"

"Great."

"Hold your judgment until after you've tasted my cooking. Your father always thought it was dreadful."

"Really? I didn't know that. Anyway, Sylvia's is terrible." Susan starts to turn red. Her stepmother used to run a catering business and is a great cook. Her mother must know that.

"How is Sylvia? And your father?"

"They're fine." Pissed off I'm here, but fine.

"Good."

Good, why good? Susan stares out the kitchen window and wonders what Edward is doing. She hears a car drive up.

"That's Lavinia," her mother says.

Susan feels nauseated. "Good," she says. "Good."

Caroline wonders if residents of Chapel Hill resent the way everything closes when the students vacate. Right now it's just an annoyance that her favorite restaurants (totally staffed by students) are closed and that there aren't any late shows at the movie houses this weekend, but she knows that on Monday the town will be back to catering to students. She can hang on till then, but what if it were permanent? She remembers how the main character in her favorite Joan Didion novel felt when she'd returned to her hometown to find that the population had dwindled to zero. Chapel Hill is a ghost town on university holidays. Even the damn library is closed. The last time Caroline stayed in town on a break, she also stayed in bed, with Edward, and she loved that they had to go to Carrboro to get a meal.

I should have known, Caroline thinks, looking at the display inside the window of the Intimate Bookshop, where the paperback edition of *Democracy* is still very prominent, that we were in trouble when Edward handed me *Play It As It Lays* and said, "So she had an abortion. I'm sure it was hell, but that's still no reason to haul the poor guy over the coals." The "poor guy" was the woman's husband and forced her to have the abortion.

The Intimate Bookshop is closed, or Caroline would go in there and kill an hour looking at all the books she hasn't read and never will and really should. Ghost town. The Revco is closed, too, which reminds her that she's out of Tampax. If nothing in the damn town opens up, she'll have to swipe her roommate's pads, which are really disgusting, because the blood sits there getting clotted in your pubic hair.

She belongs in a ghost town these days.

Before returning to Chapel Hill, Alex goes home to New York for a day. She gets money from her father, takes her sister to the new Stallone movie, which is gross, and goes out for coffee with her mother.

"How's school?"

"It's okay."

"Is Cristen still a problem?"

Alex laughs. "You could say that."

"Are you all right?"

"Yeah, I guess. I just didn't have a very good time with Celia."

"Why?"

Sometimes conversations with her mother remind Alex of the sessions she had with a psychiatrist after the rape. "I'm just not sure I like Celia too much anymore."

"Oh."

"But at the same time I'm really worried about her. I don't know... maybe I should talk to Mrs. Douglass."

"How would you feel if Celia called *me* to discuss *you?*"

Alex smiles. These conversations may be pointless, but her mother can always cut to the heart of the matter. "Yeah, but still."

"You can't be responsible for the whole world, Alex."

Celia's face flashes before Alex, next to Caroline's swollen one from that night at the police station. "Yeah, I know. I know."

13

Loose Ends

When fall break ends, Caroline feels she is being invaded. She holes up in the library between classes and only eats things that can be delivered to her room, like pizza and ice cream. This morning she notices that her eyes are pretty normal again. She should return Penelope's glasses, but since she's cutting the class they share, she isn't sure how to. That afternoon she encounters Susan standing outside the student stores looking at her watch, probably waiting for Edward, who is notorious for being late. Pulling the glasses out of her pack, Caroline taps Susan on the shoulders and watches with pleasure as she jumps and shies away.

"Would you give these to Alex when you see her?"

"Are these hers?" Susan asks.

"Just give them to her," Caroline says, walking away, feeling free and content. She does not go back to the library but sits in the grassy area between the old library and the administrative offices, where people play illegal Frisbee, hold review sessions, and generally ignore her.

That night Susan tells Edward that she has a paper to write and can't see him. She waits until her roommate goes out on her date. Then she goes down to the sorority kitchen and gets a tray of ice and a needle and thread from the housemother. In her room she holds the threaded needle over a lighted match. She places an ice cube in front of her earlobe and another in back. She sits on the bed until the ice melts, making her neck and shoulder wet and cold. She stands in front of the mirror and pushes the needle through the skin two millimeters above her already existing hole. She is surprised that there is no blood. When she has pulled the thread through, she puts one of her diamond studs in the new hole. She puts on Alex's sunglasses and looks in the mirror for a long time. She decides they make her look blind, but she likes the flashing light above her small gold hoop.

When Alex gets back to her apartment Cristen asks if she bought any new earrings because she is going out tonight.

"No. Sorry."

"Penelope called. Said she had a wild weekend."

"Oh."

"I had a lousy time. Charlotte is boh-ring."

"Sorry."

"Are you going to see Simon this week?"

"I don't know. Why, did he call?"

"No. Sorry."

Alex goes into the kitchen. She opens a Tab. "Why are you sorry?"

"That he didn't call."

Alex thinks about the flower in a Jonesfeld trash bin. "He'll call," she says.

"Sure."

The phone rings, and Alex manages to beat Cristen to it.

"Darling, did you perhaps lose it at the convent?"

Alex looks at Cristen looking at her and takes the phone into her room. "Hi, Penelope."

"You want to go out?"

"I don't know," Alex says. "I didn't do shit this weekend."

"Me neither."

Penelope is the reason I will not make dean's list, Alex thinks. "Sure," she says. "Where?"

"Molly's?"

"Okay."

Molly's is very dark, and Alex has trouble locating Penelope, who is sitting on one of the semicircular booths. Alex slips into the booth, shrugging off her pack. "I can't see a thing in here. I dropped a contact lens down the drain. If anyone smiles at us, let me know."

Penelope smiles. "Of course."

"So, tell me about your wild weekend."

"It was okay. Call it a cultural experience. How was Jonesfeld?"

"Lousy. The only highlight was that I couldn't find a place private enough to throw up."

Penelope lights a cigarette. "I thought you were going to give it up."

"Yeah. I mean to every time I do it."

"Whatever gets you through the night."

"Exactly." Alex wonders what's on her friend's mind. All the noise and smoke and beer in Molly's seems to have floated up to the dome-shaped ceiling, converging there with no intention of returning. Alex leans back in her vinyl seat and wishes that she, too, could float up there. Everyone here is drinking beer. Alex does not drink. Penelope is dragging on her cigarette. Alex does not smoke. It occurs to her that the list of what she does not do is boringly endless. Alex does not fit in, she thinks. Alex would like to be floating around the ceiling when talking to her best friend. Good.

"I want you to tell me about the rape," Penelope says.

Alex's head snaps forward.

I don't want to.

Every cunt needs a fuck.

"Caroline's." She makes it a statement of fact. "You could have heard if you hadn't left the room."

"No, not Caroline's. Yours."

Yours. Like it was something you owned. Something you could take out and examine like a possession.

"Why?"

"Why what?"

"Why do you want to know?"

"I do. I know everything except that. It makes that

seem especially more important to know." Penelope's inflection grows stronger with each "that."

"You're being very rude." Which may not be fair; perhaps Penelope only wants to reconnect, make their bond stronger now that Caroline seems to have slipped from their group. But still. "I don't want to discuss it. It's private."

"So's vomiting up every meal, and I know about that."

"That's because you walked in on me once, and I wanted to convince you it wasn't morning sickness. That was also the time, if I recall, I told you I was a virgin."

"You lied."

"Yes."

"I just want to know who. When? Where?"

Alex is quiet a moment. It is too much. No matter how she loves Penelope, she cannot overcome her own desperate desire to avoid all discussion of that night. No words will explain the sound of the waves, the smell of the strange body, how it started by her looking for brandy. No words could explain.

"It was an elephant the last time I went to the circus when I was three." She picks up her bag and strides out.

Penelope leans against the ridged back of the booth and arches her neck. She lights a cigarette. She wonders if Alex will call Caroline. The only thing worse than losing both of them would be to have them go off together without her. Shit. She does not want to think about this. She begins listening to the conversation floating over from the next booth. She half smiles. The two men are talking about sex.

"Robert, you're crazy. Ellen-Lynne has been sleeping with you for two months."

"Yeah, but I was the first."

"So, pin a medal on yourself. I'll bet the sex is just great."

"It's not like screwing a Kappa, who knows what she's doing. But Ellen-Lynne is not frigid. How do you think a girl who's been raped is going to be?"

Raped, Penelope thinks. Has everyone in the world been raped?

"I don't know. We haven't..."

"So you've been saying. Now you know why."

"A girl who's had that happen to her. How does she survive?"

"Who knows? But you don't need the headache. Come on, Simon, call Ellen-Lynne's roommate."

Penelope sits up, the smile gone. Oh, my God. Simon. Of course, if she could overhear them, they probably heard every word she and Alex said to each other. She leaves money on the table and heads for the door.

Of course, Simon will call that other girl. There are still men, especially in the South, who do not like damaged goods. Poor Alex. As soon as she gets home, she will call her and explain that it is Simon's problem and has nothing to do with her. Outside of Molly's, Penelope stops a moment. Why should she call Alex, who is probably this moment calling Caroline? If Alex can't talk to her about the rape, why should she talk to Alex about Simon? Penelope walks home in the still cold air with great purpose and satisfaction.

A week passes. And another. Alex does not talk to either Penelope, whom she is mad at, or Caroline, with whom she is not. To call Caroline would look selfish and might involve that same conversation she could not have with Penelope. Alex runs five miles every day and throws up roughly sixteen times a week. When the phone finally rings, it is not Simon, but her mother.

"Honey, I don't know how to...Celia Douglass is dead."

"Dead? What do you mean, exactly?"

"She died at Jonesfeld Memorial Hospital. She killed herself."

"Oh, no, no, no, oh, no," Alex cries across the wires into Manhattan, her tears reaching the apartment, where her mother sits helpless, able to do nothing for a twenty-year-old woman who is not sure whom she's sobbing for.

14. Recovering?

When it rains in Chapel Hill everything gets wet. Nothing is shielded. When it rains anywhere it gets wet, but in Chapel Hill the trees planted all over campus drip, adding to the sky's deluge. The red-brick buildings hold the water, swelling with moisture and mildew. The paths are slick with water and, in the fall, wet leaves. Students leave puddles in their seats and in the corridors so that it can seem there is no such thing as "dry" anywhere.

On this particular morning in October, Alex has left all three of her umbrellas in the bottom of her closet. *Singin' in the Rain* was a movie she and Celia used to wait up for once they got old enough to see the late show. Alex thought it might make her feel better to prance to class unprotected. It hasn't.

When she gets to Greenlaw building, she goes directly to the bathroom to dry herself off with the brown scratchy towels the restrooms always have. In the small, silver-framed mirror hanging six inches above the sink, a stranger looks out. She is not wearing any earrings, her shoulders are thrown forward instead of back, and she is very, very wet. No wonder she's hunched forward; the sweater must weigh a ton. Alex tries to wring some water out of her hair and only succeeds in getting her notebooks wet. It's hopeless. Clean dry hair and a matching sweater will not conjure up Celia any more than the umbrellaless walk did. She starts down to the hall, and at the exit sign Edward catches up with her.

"Hullo, my own favorite city."

"Oh, hi."

"Oh, hi? I must be slipping. That almost always gets some kind of reaction."

"Go away," she says. "I have class."

"No. I don't think so." He puts an arm around her gingerly—she is, after all, soaking—and says, "Alex, dear, come with me, and I shall buy you a cup of coffee."

She smiles, not totally, but wide enough to show her incisors. "Oh, Edward, would you? It seems such a long time since I've had coffee with anyone."

"Now tell me," he says a little later, bringing her a steamy Styrofoam cup, "What's wrong with my sunny friend?"

There are already teethmarks on Alex's cup, and when

she finishes she will tear it to little pieces, leaving a white mound behind her.

"A friend, one of my very best, died," she says.

She looks at his face. It is panic stricken. "No, not one of my best friends you know. Celia. Celia Douglass. And the worst of it is is that when I last saw her we had a fight over which one of us had screwed more men."

"Ah, come now, Alex, that didn't kill her."

"No, I know. She killed her. She killed herself."

"Suicide?"

"Yes. Think how unhappy you have to be to do that. How alone. And I should have seen it; there was no way she could have been connected to anyone there. Fucking northeastern convent."

"You know, Alex, I did meet her a couple of times. At parties in New York, and later, seeing who your friends were here, I thought it was funny that you should be friends."

"All through high school...she was there. Always," Alex says quietly.

"I'm sorry. What can I do?"

"Nothing. You're doing it."

"Have you told Penelope?"

"I haven't told Miss Samms shit for two weeks."

"So, it's true, then?"

"What is?"

"You're not speaking."

"How do you know that?"

"Bullfoot grapevine."

"Well, it's right for once."

"Why?"

There's no way of telling him without bringing in the

rape, and she cannot dump that on him on top of Celia.

"It's nothing. You know, Edward, your girl isn't so bad after all." She owes him something, and this is what pops to mind. "She thinks I'm pretty," Alex adds with a laugh.

"You are," Edward says lightly.

"Right."

"Alex..."

She looks up at him. Go ahead, her expression says, make my day.

"Forget it."

"Oh, Christ," Alex says. "Here comes Cristen."

Edward looks up. "Sweetie, I have to run, but I want you to call me when it gets bad. Is that a promise?" He is gathering up his coat and books.

"Oh, yes, I guess. Thank you."

He lays his damp umbrella on the table. "Just keep this for the rest of the day, okay?"

"No, Edward, I can't...." It's too late, he's gone, and into his seat plumps Cristen.

"You look terrible. I told you to take an umbrella."

"Thanks, Mom."

"Alex, Penelope will come around."

Alex glances up sharply.

Penelope, Penelope. There was a time, Alex thinks, when Penelope might have fixed this injury, this death that feels as if her soul has been excised. She will never replace Penelope and realizes that now Celia must be replaced, and it will be impossible.

"Yes, I suppose," she tells Cristen listlessly.

"Look, I'll clean up everything today." The mess has gotten worse than usual, and the apartment needs a premature spring cleaning.

"Thanks, Cristen, I appreciate it."

"No problem." Cristen takes one of the Styrofoam pieces Alex has just discarded and rolls it around her fingers. Alex can tell Cristen would really like to help, but what would be the point? She does not want to explain that the problem is Celia, not Penelope. If she doesn't talk about it, it will go away.

Cristen gets up—lumbers, really—and says, "See you later."

Alex watches Cristen's bulk disappear. "Bye," she whispers.

Edward grips Susan by the elbow and steers her toward the doorway of the cafeteria, where students and soggy faculty members are streaming in and out. "Come on, baby, Alex doesn't want any company now."

"Edward, let go of me. I have something to give her."

"Not today you don't."

"Why not?"

"A friend of hers from home just died. Suicide."

"How awful. Edward, let go of me. I want to tell her I'm sorry."

"Later."

"Edward, Alexandria is a friend of mine, and if I want to go over there, I will."

"A friend of yours?"

"Yes!"

"Look, you stupid bitch, she hates your guts."

Susan wrenches free from Edward's grasp and stares at him. Stupid bitch? Okay, stupid she can deal with, anyone after Caroline would be stupid, but bitch? That's excessive.

"Susan, I'm sorry, I, I, had no right."

"Forget it."

He starts to walk away.

"Just one thing, Edward."

"Yes?"

"Why does she hate me?"

Edward sits down on a seat by the exit; it's wet. "Come here," he says, motioning to his lap.

She does; habits die hard.

"I think because, once, a very long time ago, I took her out."

"You always take her out."

"Susan, don't be dense, huh?"

"Oh. How could you have stopped seeing her? I never would have."

"She's a very tough girl."

"I'm not?"

"No, you're not."

"What's wrong with being tough?"

"I'm afraid I can't tell you, but I have an idea from watching my Amazons that being tough is being lonely."

Lonely. He doesn't think she's lonely when he's babbling about parliamentary systems? What does he think it feels like to lie under him, counting backward from one hundred waiting for him to finish?

"Edward, I think you're wrong. She doesn't hate me."

He shrugs. "Have it your own way, then."

"I will."

"Alexandria?"

Alex looks up. Susan is standing, dripping just a little, and holding Penelope's sunglasses the way a bride holds her bouquet, very tight and proud.

"Yes?"

"I'm so sorry about Edward. I didn't know."

"Know what?"

"That you had a thing for him. Once."

Susan is amazed that Alexandria starts to laugh.

"Sit down," Alexandria says. "Do you realize that if I remembered every guy who's given me the run around and then avoided all their girlfriends, I'd have no one on campus to talk to?"

Susan suddenly remembers that yes, Alexandria and Caroline are very good friends. "Here, these are yours." She puts the glasses on the tabletop.

"No, they're Penelope's."

Susan touches her diamond stud. "Caroline told me to give them to you."

"Yes, well, thanks."

"You're welcome." Susan starts to get up.

"Would you like to come over tonight?" Alex asks.

"Me?"

Alex looks around the cafeteria. "Yes."

"Sure. What time?"

"Ten?"

"Great. Bye." Susan has two tests tomorrow and no clean clothes, but she can't remember the last time she was so excited.

The night sky is streaked with dark purple clouds. Alex watches from the apartment's balcony as the silvery after-rain moon breaks through the muted colors. The air is clean and fresh, smelling like new-mown wet grass. She was going to ask Celia to come down next semester and serve a Penelope-style tea on the balcony.

When the door knocks, Alex knows it's not Susan. Susan is not the type of girl who shows up early.

"Yes?"

"Alex, will you let me in?" It's Penelope.

Alex opens the door. "Hi. My God, what's the matter?" Penelope's mascara has caked underneath her eyes, which are red, and her hair looks all hacked up, as if someone combed it with an egg beater.

"That's what I was going to ask you. Is there something wrong with me?"

"Of course not." Alex makes a space on the couch. "Here, sit down."

"Oh, Alex, I'm so unhappy. And sorry."

Apologies Alex can deal with later. "Colin?"

"Yes. This afternoon I bring him flowers for the opening of his damn play, and he informs me that I'm a very nice girl, but he's just not attracted to me."

"Of course he isn't. He's gay."

"I know, I know. But it's always gay men. Or sleazy men. What am I? A masochist? A fag hag?"

Alex gets up and turns off the stereo. "Let the Sunshine In" is not really appropriate right now. "No, I don't think you're a fag hag. From what I understand, a fag hag seeks out the company of gay men. Colin hit on you first."

"But why'd I let him? I've been through this a million times. There is no future in a queer."

Alex goes to the kitchen and gets two Tabs. Handing one to Penelope, she thinks about the collage on her friend's wall: Polo ads for Ralph Lauren of people lying on the beach in mismatched clothes; men posing for Calvin Klein perfume wearing nothing, or nothing but Calvin Klein underwear.

"Maybe," she says slowly, "what somebody looks like is just too important to you."

"Of course it's important to me," Penelope snaps, wiping her eyes with her white T-shirt. "You think what I look like isn't important to them?"

"I don't know. It's hard to judge. I'd love you no matter what you looked like. I love you right now, and you're a mess."

Penelope laughs. "I cut my hair with a pair of nail scissors."

"So I see. Any particular reason?"

"I guess I wanted a concrete reason to hate myself."

"Next time try throwing up. It's more destructive, and the results aren't as apparent."

"They will be."

"I know."

"You'd better watch it. I read just the other day about a woman who did it so much it started happening spontaneously; she couldn't control it."

"Did you come here to discuss my puking?"

"Not really, but you do it because you care about what you look like, so don't tell *me* that I care too much what people look like."

You're wrong, Alex thinks. I do it because sometimes I feel so empty I have to fill that void, but I can't stand to be fat. I'm a fucking psycho.

"Okay," she says.

"Alex?"

"Yes?"

"I'm sorry about that night."

"Forget it."

"I just feel useless sometimes, and getting you to talk to me makes it better."

"I know."

"Alex?"

"Yes?"

"Why couldn't you've been a man?"

"I don't know, Penelope. Next time around I'll give it my best shot."

"Would you really want to be? I mean, I'd love if you were because it would solve my love life, but I'd hate to be a man myself."

"I wouldn't. If I were a guy, nobody'd ever have raped me. I wouldn't get thought of as a second-class citizen just because I bleed twelve times a year."

"You know, I think if faggots got the curse, it would cure them faster than you can say 'fairy.'"

"Perhaps."

"I really liked him."

"I know."

"Was being raped that horrid?"

"Yes. It's like failing a test you studied all night for. You feel like you're so dumb not to have been strong enough to stand on your feet. It's . . . Being raped is from hunger."

"From hunger, huh? That sounds like something Susan would say."

"Susan! Christ, what time is it?"

Penelope looks at her wrist. "Nine-forty. Why?"

"Susan's coming over at ten."

"Good Lord. Why on earth?"

"I asked her to."

"Alexandria Rust, have you lost your marbles?"

"Yes, maybe. But look, I've given you fair warning. So if you want to take off, no hard feelings."

"Thank you, darling. I'll certainly clear out before the plague descends. Mind if I go repair myself?"

"No, go ahead."

Alex neatens the pile of *Tar Heels* on her couch. Decides they look better messy and spreads them around.

When Penelope reemerges, she is her usual immaculate self; her hair just looks a little punkier.

"You want another Tab?" Alex asks.

"Yeah, why not?"

"No particular reason except they're Cristen's."

"I'll drink it just so long I don't have to take another midnight ride to Raleigh to replace them."

Alex laughs and puts the stereo back on. "Bowie okay?"

"Sure. You have 'Changes One'?"

"Of course."

The girls sit on the floor reading the album's liner notes.

"You know," Alex says, "I really thought Simon would turn out to be the 'innocent man.'"

"You mean he hasn't called you?" Penelope's voice is a little stiff.

"Nope."

"Men can just be that way, Alex. Don't feel bad."

"I don't. I remember this song my little sister taught me once. 'All men are bastards, and if you ever forget it, one will always remind you.'"

Penelope giggles. "Did I ever tell you about the time I informed my father that I might be a bastard?"

"Why did you do that?"

"To see his face change colors. I don't know. The time I got him best, though, was when I was about six. He came to pick me up from nursery school, and right before he entered the playground I climbed up the jungle gym and hollered, 'My daddy sells vacuum bags.' He yelled all the way home."

"Did you even know," Alexandria asks, "what a vacuum cleaner was?"

"I don't think so. I was just testing the waters. Poor Daddy."

"Indeed."

"Bloody hell, it's almost ten. Let me get out of here before Mata Hari descends."

"Bye."

"Bye. And darling..." Penelope stops at the door.

"Yes?"

"Thanks."

"It was a pleasure."

"Maybe I'll even try and patch up with Caroline. Make this my good works day."

"Good night, Penelope."

"Good night, sweet princess, and may flights of—"

"Yeah, yeah, spare me."

"Bye."

Caroline is lying on her bed, her feet propped up on the iron posts, her eyes staring at the cinder-block walls. Her roommate is at a chapter meeting; outside on the volleyball court the new pledges of a black fraternity are doing a step show. So it's October, Caroline thinks, when the Fascist mood runs rampant and young black boys goosestep around campus as part of their initiation rites.

She sits up, swinging her feet to the floor with a plop. I guess it's no worse than the pledge class in Edward's fraternity last year who stole the frat house's front door and acted as though it was the cleverest thing since the Zimmerman telegram. She kicks an empty pizza box across the floor. It has not been a good day. Ducking into the cafeteria to seek refuge from the rain, what should she see but the lovely tableau of Susan sitting on Edward's lap. After purchasing a badly needed cup of coffee, she was assaulted by the sight of her ex-best friend and Susan, who had miraculously detached herself from Edward, deep in conversation.

Maybe Alex has a thing for pretty girls, too, now. Maybe it's catching. Right. And maybe Susan is a dyke. Wouldn't that be precious? If Edward came back to her because his current flame fell for *her* best friend. She wishes she could bring herself to talk to Penelope, but she cannot put out of mind the erect, disapproving back of her friend the night of her endless ride from Durham. Shit. No Edward. No Alex. No Penelope. No more Amazons. She cannot think of a reason for staying here. She has not been the greatest of classgoers, her umbrella is broken, and she is tired of eating pizza. She has to make an appearance in court, but not for another two weeks. Thanks to Alex's father she has her car, and, sober, she doesn't really need her license; cops will be unlikely to stop her.

Caroline gets her keys from the faded jeans jacket she wore to Durham that night and has not touched since and the letter her parents sent her detailing their last trip to Washington. She checks her wallet—sixty dollars. She will stop at the bank machine and get a hundred more. She takes her blue wool coat from the closet's top shelf. She looks around the stark room.

"Good-bye," she whispers.

She is going to see her brother.

15.

Pilgrimage

When Penelope leaves Alex's apartment complex, she decides not to return to Carr Street; instead she heads toward South Campus. The lobby of Morrison is gray but bathed in yellow light. Girls in bathrobes and curlers are coming out of the snack bar carrying Tabs and bags of Cheetos. Some guys are playing hockey, using one of the elevators for their goal post. She holds on to her bag tightly; this place reminds her of Port Authority. The elevator comes, and she bolts for the back corner, amazed at all the people who can fit in.

There's no answer at Caroline's door. She thinks about leaving a note on the Pi Phi message board but decides against it. Coming out of the suite, she hears her name called.

"Hi, Greg." Just what she needs tonight. Greg Neals, famous drama department Casanova, a friend of Colin's. She ignores the gray eyes and turns to go.

"What brings your fair face down to these parts?"

What the fuck does he care? "Just looking for a friend."

"Well, it's your lucky night, lovely Penelope. Here I am." He is grinning, his arms spread wide.

All he needs is a big red bow and I'll take it. "What happened? Couldn't corrupt the morals of a new crush as easily as you did me?"

"Oh, Penelope you weren't a corruption, you were fun."

"Thank you very much." She heads for the elevators again. A little more determined this time. She thinks.

"So what's the big rush?"

"The rush, Greg darling, is that there's no future with you and me. . . . "

She stops; he had put his hand right between her legs and the other on her left breast and is whispering, "No future, honey, but one hell of a fun present."

Well, he's got her there. Her body tells her it's been too long, too damn long. That voice in her head says, "Not again! Somewhere out there is a nice man, and he's looking for you."

Penelope removes Greg's hand from her breast, but he's got a visor lock on her crotch. "Lead the way, darling," she says.

His room is an exact replica of the one she and Terry

shared last year, the one Caroline and Alex shared. She wishes she could just lose herself to the sensation of his tongue running around the rim of her ear and his hand slowly making its way up to her bra hook, but she's not into it. He must be an R.A., she thinks. In Morrison only resident assistants have singles, and there is only one bed in this room. How funny that she didn't know that. It occurs to her that last semester she and Greg didn't talk a lot, so it's not that funny. They spent a lot of time in bed, and that's what men like Greg Neals are good for. You don't talk, laugh, or cry with them. You have Amazons for that. Greg Neals is for fucking, and she pushes him down onto the bed.

When Caroline switches on the ignition, her car radio blasts forth. "He bop, she bop, and we bop," screeches out Cyndi Lauper. Grimacing, Caroline turns off the volume. It reminds her that the last time she was in this car was with that creep from Durham. Bob. French-talking babies, he told her, when through her drunken haze she managed to babble out that she was no longer on the pill.

"No problem, pretty girl. We'll have some French-talking babies."

That's when she started to fight. That's when he punched her in the face. That's when she managed to throw him out, get in the driver's seat, and the screaming lights of a police car drove her off the road. Into a tree. And nobody had turned off the radio. That's the kind of thing Carl would have laughed at.

Carl. Caroline and Carl. Her parents were sure cute when they named their kids. He'd be thirty-one this year; he might have married Nina, who cried for a few months, then married a garage mechanic and now has two kids. Sometimes Caroline goes to see her on her vacations home, but not too often. She should have swiped some of Deena Jane's No-Doz. This is going to be a long trip.

When Penelope leaves, Alex throws the empty Tab cans away and puts Bowie's "Let's Dance" on the stereo. Alex would like to look like David Bowie. All angular and eerily beautiful. Alex will never forgive her father for marrying into a family with hippy, busty women. The fact that at the time of her parents' wedding every man in the world wanted to screw Kim Novak totally escapes her. She would like to be Twiggy. She will settle for Susan, who is at the door.

"Hi."

"Hi, come in."

"Thanks."

This is going to be a great conversation.

"Can I sit here?" Susan motions to a corner of the couch.

"Of course. Sure. Anywhere."

"Are you feeling better?"

"What do you mean?"

"About your friend.... Edward told me."

Celia, Celia, you should have called me, Celia. "Oh, yeah, I guess. I had no idea she was so unhappy."

"Oh. Had you seen her recently?"

"Yeah. Fall break. I had a lousy time. I guess that's a terrible thing to say."

"No. I went to see my mother and had a worse time than you can possibly imagine."

Alex laughs. "Well, going home is rarely fun."

"I said I went to see my mother, not home."

"Oh." Alex pauses a minute. "Weird. You mean your father got custody?"

"Yes."

"That's funny. I remember how in the seventh grade everyone was getting a bar mitzvah, or their parents were splitting. I was really out of it. Anyway, most of the kids went with Mommy or had to split the week—you know, joint custody."

"My mother ran away with another woman. She didn't stand a chance in court." Susan blurts this out, and Alex wonders if it's not an exchange for the news of Celia.

"Really? Neat. I mean, well, it's different, anyway." Cristen would be glad to see Alex at a loss for words.

"Different," Susan repeats woodenly.

"Is that why you had a lousy time? Is it the first time you've seen her?"

"No." Susan puts her add-a-beads in her mouth and spits them out again. "No. It was just the first time that I understood why she left. She really loves that woman. The way you love a man, you know?"

Alex has never loved a man; she does not know. "Do you love Edward?" she asks all in a rush.

"Yes, yes, of course. I wouldn't sleep with him otherwise."

"Really?"

"Yes. Really."

"I'm just curious, you see; Caroline slept with him before she loved him, and Penelope sleeps with lots of people she doesn't love, so I don't always grasp the connection."

Susan looks at her blankly.

"Between sex and love, I mean."

"Do you sleep with people you don't love?"

Every cunt needs a fuck.

I don't want to.

"Yes."

"Would you sleep with a woman?"

Alex thinks of one of the leather jackets drinking coffee at the Jonesfeld cafeteria. She thinks about David Bowie in a dress. Does that count?

"I don't know." She sounds too serious. With a laugh: "Is this a proposition?"

Susan watches the lamplight throw its glow to the gold dangling from Alexandria's ears. She looks at the long legs curled up under some old *Tar Heel*s. She wonders about heredity. She thinks about Edward, her sorority.

"No," she says. "Just curious."

"Ricochet, ricochet, it's not the end of the world," growls Bowie from the stereo.

Welcome to Norfolk. Oh, goody. There's no way she'll stay up for the two or three hours necessary to make it to D.C. Caroline heads off the freeway. Cruising the city for a cheap motel, she spots an empty parking lot. She will lock all the car doors and pray nobody bothers her. She stretches out, as much as her six-foot frame will let her, in the backseat and tries to sleep.

She remembers the funeral—the American flag draped over the coffin, her new Mary Janes that gave her a blister, and the silent, unmoving figure of her weeping father. Her mother didn't shed a tear but spent the next day packing up Carl's room and driving the boxes over to the Salvation Army. Caroline filched her brother's track trophy. She'd always remember him that way—sweaty and musky smelling, tousling her hair and giving Nina, who'd brought her along for a treat, a big kiss. When I grow up, Caroline had thought, I want to be kissed just like that: hard and in front of a lot of people.

She sighs and repositions her head against the car's arm rest. I still do.

Penelope leans over Greg's sleeping form and takes a cigarette from his pack by the clock radio. She exhales, trying to make a smoke ring. She has never been fucked from behind before. She is not sure that it made sleeping with him worth it. She can still hear Colin saying, "You're a very nice girl, Penelope, but . . ." She sighs and thinks about getting dressed, but maybe Greg will wake up and tell her she's lovely and to please stay, it makes a difference. "And maybe, Miss Samms, you're the bleedin' queen of England."

When Caroline wakes up, the green glow on her dashboard says it's five-thirty. Her neck hurts, and her throat is dry and scratchy. She buys a Coke when she stops for gas and then hightails it out of Norfolk. She would kill or die for a shower. Kill or die. One of Penelope's sayings. She wonders how things are going with Colin. "That girl needs a man," Caroline sings out. That's the nice thing about being in a car; no one looks at you funny even when you deserve it. The car has become a very visible manifestation of the invisible wall she has been longing to build around her since that night at O'Grady's. She sings out again to test her newfound freedom and then grimaces. For Christ's sake, why does any girl need a man? Maybe her brother could have answered that. Maybe he still can. No one alive that Caroline knows can. She turns on the radio. Cyndi Lauper again, crooning "Time After Time." Caroline sings along, really belting it out. Carl used to say he was tone deaf, maybe he had a punctured eardrum, be a four F. So he fucking enlisted to find out. Enlisted. Couldn't even wait for his draft number. "Was it that bad, O brother of mine? Was it as bad for you as it is for me?"

Susan meets Edward for breakfast. She called him last night after getting back from Alex's. "Eight-thirty," she said. "Waffle shop." Well, that was dumb. There are always a million people at the waffle shop, and the waitresses hurry you, and the counters are greasy, and the air smells like fried eggs. Not a good place to tell someone you want to break up.

"Okay," he says, wiping his plate with whole-wheat toast. "How come?"

I love your best friend. "You called me a stupid bitch," she whispers, aware of the two girls at the very close next table.

"I apologized for that. And I meant it."

"You don't respect me," Susan supplements.

Edward starts to laugh. "God in hell. Women. Caroline used to tell me I respected her as a person, but not as a woman. What do you want, Susan? For me to admire the job you do on desk duty? Give me a break."

She stares at him wordlessly. Caroline, always Caroline. Those goddamn fucking Amazons. She remembers suddenly that Alexandria is an Amazon and bites her lip.

"Look," he says, staring at her mouth, "you're a very pretty girl, but I'll be goddamned if you get me to say more than that." He puts ten dollars on the table. "This should cover it," he says, pushing back his chair. He slams out of the restaurant, and the door makes the little silver sound it always makes when someone leaves.

Susan takes the ten dollars and brings the check to the cash register. Pocketing her change, she wonders how much those girls heard. She leaves, forgetting, until she gets back to the sorority, that she didn't leave a tip. She never forgets that.

Penelope climbs the steps to her room softly. She doesn't want any of her housemates to wake and beat her to the bathroom. She needs a shower. A shower to beat down on her neck and a thick white bar of Ivory to make her new and fresh. Like a virgin, as Madonna sings. She stands naked on the cold tile floor, waiting for the water to warm up. Rubbing her thighs together to ward off the chill, she is suddenly aware of the thick stickiness in and around her crotch. Oh, Christ, my diaphragm's in my closet; and he didn't use anything. She jumps in the shower and scrubs her vagina with soap. She'd like some peroxide, a douche, a bidet. Anything. A wire hanger? How could she have been so stupid? What was that pill called Caroline and Alex talked about? A DES. She'd have to call student health, which is always a royal drag, and anyway you don't get pregnant from one night. That would be ridiculous. She stops her scrubbing and lets the water beat down on her back.

When Caroline finally reaches the Vietnam memorial, after circling Dupont Circle four times trying to find someone to give her directions, she is struck by the neatly kept grass sprawling before the black marble. They could hold Wimbledon here, she thinks, taking her parents' letter out of her pack.

"It was truly lovely. . . . Carl is on 42E, you would be proud."

The memorial starts out low, the first piece very small, holding one name, and then the onslaught comes. Each piece gets larger, covered with more and more names. The two sides converge in the right angle of two slabs larger than Titans. Caroline stands in front of that corner. There are American flags and flowers in front of some of the pieces. Some people are strolling by, some are walking with a purpose. She sees an old woman reach out and caress a name. Caroline turns before she has to witness the reaction of the woman's realization that her son's life has come down to an engraved name in a strange city, amid a sea of such engravings. She starts walking east, hunting for block 42. The blocks are scaling down in size now, and number 42 is just about her height. She can see herself, clumsy and dirty looking, out of place even here. She starts scanning the names, and there he is; in the bottom left-hand corner sandwiched between Thimothy Schroeder and Edward A. Schultz—Carl R. Schrombs.

She should have brought him something and the sun is burning her neck and she wants to have by her the flesh and blood of these neat smooth letters that spell Carl R. Schrombs. Caroline sits on her pack and studies her brother's name for a while. Then she pulls out a pencil and piece of notebook paper and makes a rubbing. The paper does not tear as she places it over his name and sketches the pencil over the surface. "der Carl R. Schrombs Edwa," it reads. Standing, she folds the paper and slips it in her back pocket. Not until she reaches the Lincoln Memorial and climbs the big, plantationlike steps, and looks up at the huge statue, does she cry. She cries and thinks how nice and safe it would be to curl up in Lincoln's marble lap, sleep, and disappear.

16.

Edward's Girl

When Caroline gets back to Chapel Hill, after one week in Washington waiting for her $160 to run out, she hangs her rubbing on the wall. She stays in bed for three weeks staring at the wall. Her roommate spends more and more time at the sorority house and suggests that maybe Caroline go to student health. Yes, well.

Finally, it is the approach of Thanksgiving that drives Caroline from her bed. She is in danger of sleeping through it. She has never slept through a holiday before, and it occurs to her that if she doesn't lay off the Valium, she may sleep through them all.

One of the first things she does on campus, while cutting the class she has with Penelope, is go to the student stores. In the back, past the aisles holding clean notebooks, tape, and multicolored pens, and before the small carpeted bookstore that sells J. D. Salinger stories and essays of literary criticism, there is a corner full of stiff paperback guides to LSATs, GREs, and colleges. Caroline pulls out the *Yale Insider's Guide to Colleges,* her Bible in twelfth grade. She skims the introduction—"Liberal versus Conservative," "High Tech Hits Higher Ed," "Colleges with Beautiful Campuses"—and then flips to Pennsylvania, her favorite state. Bryn Mawr, no; Drexel University, no; Haverford, maybe. No fraternities or sororities, deadline January 31. Transfers accepted: fifteen. Well, bag that. U of P, a definite maybe; University of Pittsburgh, no thanks; Swarthmore? Who knows? She'd better take this someplace where the lights aren't so bright, where the print won't swim around in a blur.

Coming out of the glass double doors, she sees Penelope sitting across the Pit on the steps; she is flipping frantically through a red book. Caroline thinks about going over and saying, "Hi, what's up?" as though she had been asking that every day for the past month. No, she thinks, holding her new book, her passport out. One thing at a time.

Penelope is waiting for Alex and going through her datebook. Okay, that small "p" in the upper-right corner of the square labeled October 2 means her last period started then. So she's twelve days overdue. No biggie, that happens. Alex hasn't had her period in a year, what with all that puking. But *shit!!* She doesn't puke, and she's never been late; she has always been regular since she was twelve and in the sixth grade and one of her sisters took her into the bathroom with a hand mirror and a box of tampons and showed her how to insert one. It took an hour to learn, but she's never ever been late or missed. Shit, shit, shit.

Two hands cover her eyes.

"Hello, Alex."

"How did you ever know it was me?" Alex demands, sitting down with a little tinkling sound.

Too many fucking earrings. "Just lucky, I guess." Lucky, fucking lucky.

"Was that Caroline over across the Pit?" Alex asks.

"I didn't see anyone," Penelope answers. "But then I haven't seen her in so long it's quite possible that I wouldn't recognize her."

"Yeah, me neither. I wonder if she's mad at me."

"Who cares? I can't deal with her prima donna act."

"So, what's up?"

Me, Penelope thinks. Penelope Samms, vacuum cleaner queen, ambassador's daughter, knocked up; but Alex doesn't know about Greg, and Penelope doesn't want to discuss it.

"Nothing, how about you?" It is not a question; she does not care. Does not give a fuck. A fuck, a fuck. How can a baby come from just a fuck?

"Well, let's see. Cristen is very happy that we're talking again, when am I going to call Caroline, how come I talk to Susan Simmons, and am I dating Edward?"

"Are you?"

"Am I what? Talking to Susan or dating Edward?"

"Both, I guess. Are you doing both, darling?"

"Yes to Susan, no to Edward, but he's been coming around an awful lot. I think I should be insulted; he's got all this free time now that he's not banging Susan, and I'm a convenient old shoe until the next pretty girl comes along."

Penelope has no answer. Alex always thinks she should be insulted, and who knows, maybe she should.

"Edward," Alex says, pushing her empty plate away. "You were not jerking me around. You sure can cook."

"My talents are wide and varied," he says with a smile.

She's stuffed and thinks about asking for a glass of milk, but maybe the ice cream will work.

"Where's the bathroom?"

"Top of the stairs to your left."

Not a moment too soon. Her skin is beginning to crawl.

"Alex?"

She stops at the landing. "Yes?"

"Are you going to puke up my lovely dinner?"

God damn Caroline to hell. If I ever see her again . . .

"Yes, I guess I am, but don't worry, I'm a pro. I never make a mess."

He is on her in a flash. "No, no, you're not. Chronic vomiting can rupture blood vessels, decay your teeth, and eat through your stomach lining. It can also give you a heart attack."

"What do you know?"

"I don't often spend a whole afternoon in the library for nothing."

What's wrong with him? Why would he bother looking all that stuff up? It doesn't matter. She needs desperately to get upstairs to the bathroom. "Chronic eating also makes you fat," she shoots back. "Edward, take your hands off me. All that poison you fed me is going to digest if I don't get to the bathroom."

"Alex, this is one meal you're keeping."

"No, it is not."

She tries to break free of his grasp and, when she can't, kicks his legs. She's in good shape, but he's bigger and picks her up and places her on the chair she has just bolted from.

"You're staying here for half an hour, until you won't be able to."

He's serious, he's fucking serious. The sugar from the ice cream is racing around her bloodstream; the meat and vegetables are expanding; in a minute she's going to be a blimp. Her skin feels hot and oily. She's so damn unclean.

"Edward, why are you doing this to me?" His eyes are like the mirrors she has spent so much of her life avoiding; they reflect back what is there and what she sees all at once, making it impossible to get a decent view. She tries to conjure up an image that might be his: fierce staring eyes, silly earrings, broad shoulders, a long neck.

Breaking through her thoughts and physical illness at holding in all this food is his voice, and it is saying, "Alexandria, I love you."

He has said that he loves her, and Alex knows that with men, love leads to this. That is why she is lying in his bed. A bed that has held Caroline (making Alex feel sad and disloyal) and Susan (making her feel smug and self-satisfied).

She is amazed that she is not nervous. Just her muscles are tight, tight as if after a run. It makes her feel good to know that with one swift motion of her knee and a quick run she can arrive at safety, leaving him completely incapacitated. Her muscles tighten some more.

"Turn over," he says.

What the hell? She does.

Starting at her neck, Edward rubs her back, very gently, the way her mother did when she had a fever.

"Edward?"

"Hmm?"

"Do you like the beach?"

He kisses her shoulder, keeps rubbing her back. "Why?"

"I do. We had a house there. Once. My father sold it."

"Did you go on weekends or just summers?"

"Mostly summers, but when Mommy was in medical school my father would take Nicole and me on weekends so she could stay in the city and study."

"Oh." He turns her over and, smiling, begins to take her earrings out, one by one by one. They are the slip-in kind with no backs.

"Do you ever miss New York?" she asks.

"Sometimes. Not around you." He kisses her, moves his mouth to her shoulder, her breast, back to her face.

"Don't be afraid, Alex. I won't let anything happen to you."

She runs her hands down his arms. She is a lot of things right now, but afraid is not one of them.

17. What They're Eating

Susan is eating fruitcake. She is sitting on her bed in a room in a house full of women eating fruitcake she got on sale at the supermarket. She hoped it would put her in the mood for the holidays. Before her are white papers covered with blue ink; they are letters from her parents.

"Susan, I don't think it's necessary to point out that you have always spent Thanksgiving with Sylvia and me. No one could be more happy than I that you are speaking to your mother, but enough's enough." From her father.

"And while it was lovely to see you in October, it was

far too short, and I feel like I've approached an iceberg that's barely been touched. Please, honey, it would be so nice if you spent Thanksgiving with me." From her mother.

The fruitcake is not working, and Susan pushes the papers from her bed, where they float under the various desks and bureaus in the room. Fuck it. Maybe she'll just stay here and ponder where to go for Christmas. In September she thought that Edward might ask her along to New York. Well, talk about counting your chickens. She ditches Edward for Alexandria, and the two of them are living happily ever after.

Did she ditch Edward for Alex? Is she a lesbian? Can she be cured? Is there anyone she can ask? She's afraid of giving her father cardiac arrest and equally afraid of how pleased her mother would be at the news.

Putting the last piece of cake in her mouth, Susan crosses the room to her dresser. She flips through the Chapel Hill directory until she gets to Mental Health: 555-2281.

"Mental Health."

"Um, hi. I'd like to make an appointment. To see someone."

"Well, let's see. I have an opening on Tuesday at twelve."

"That's fine."

"If it's an emergency..."

"No, no. Tuesday's fine. Really. That's great."

Does she sound like an emergency?

Alex stands in front of the produce section in Fowler's, the white clapboard supermarket on Franklin Street. She is surveying the grapes and thinking, If I eat another grape, I'm going to puke.

But she's promised Edward she won't vomit anymore, so now she's eating grapes. Just grapes and nothing else. They fill you up and then go right through you. It's one way of staying thin without upchucking, but it sure is boring. She loads up her blue plastic basket with red, purple, and white seedless. You got to get your variety where you can. She goes to the express line. She has to meet Edward in half an hour. He is driving her out to University Lake.

"The crew team works out here in the mornings," Edward tells her as she dumps the contents of her bookbag out onto a wooden dock. The lake is surrounded by a scraggly grass bank and boats of all variety are stacked under the docks. It is one of those ridiculously warm winter days that make studying so hard.

"The really industrious ones run out to the lake and back in order to increase the level of their training."

"How do you know?" Alex asks, searching for her copy of *To the Lighthouse.*

"My roommate last year was on the team."

"Yeah, Caroline said he went to bed very early. . . ." She trails off and looks at him helplessly.

"It's okay," he says.

Hurriedly, Alex begins to speak. "I have to figure out why Virginia Woolf is more modern than Margaret Drabble. I wish Penelope had done the reading. We could talk about it endlessly."

"It's easy. I'll tell you why. I took the same course last year."

"I think I'm going to say that Woolf strives to reconcile structure and image, and Drabble doesn't even know they need to be brought together."

"That's not what I said in my paper."

"What did you get?"

"B plus."

"I'll get an A. I guarantee it."

"Jesus, Alex. I can occasionally be useful. I coached Susan through two econ. midterms."

She stretches out on the grass, stares up at the pale sky. "How unfortunate for you that I can think for myself."

He decides to laugh. "Sorry I offered."

"What's your favorite street at home?" she asks.

"Twenty-third."

"Mine's Fifty-seventh. You can buy three pairs of earrings for five dollars all up and down Fifty-seventh."

"Oh," he says, making small circles on her hand with two of his fingers.

"Favorite housepet?"

"Doberman."

"Like fun."

"What's yours?"

"Garter snake," she says, and sticks her tongue out at him.

"Favorite color?" he asks.

"Brown."

"Why?"

"My hair is brown."

"Oh, Alex, your hair is too many different colors to be captured by 'brown.'" He pulls her up from the ground so that he can sit behind her, his chin leaning on her left shoulder.

"It says brown on my passport. What are you talking about?"

"Have you ever really looked at it?" he asks. "It's dark and light, and each shade has a different color. It's beautiful."

"I'm glad something is."

"I wish I knew how you got to have such a queer idea of what you look like. I wish I could fix it."

She pulls away and stares at him. "Favorite singer," she snaps.

"Springsteen."

"Just checking," she says.

"Yours?"

"Billy Joel." She drags the name out slowly, pronouncing it the way Penelope might. "Billy Joel."

The day Caroline drops her applications in the mail (U of P, Swarthmore, and, as an afterthought, Berkeley), she decides to go see Penelope. Despite everything, she will miss her funny foreign friend, with her penchant for gay men and Amazons. The small house on Carr Street is unusually quiet. No loud music, no girls lounging outside or having tea. Caroline enters through the always open back door. Once inside the kitchen she can hear the unmistakable sounds of someone throwing up in the adjoining bathroom.

Penelope comes into the kitchen wiping her face with a damp terry towel.

"Caroline!"

"Hi, the door was open, and I didn't..." Caroline trails off. Penelope looks horrible, and Caroline feels as though she is treading in very private waters. She does not leave;

at one time she loved Penelope very much.

"Are you okay?"

Penelope goes to the stove and puts the kettle on. She sits on one of the wooden chairs and pulls one out for Caroline.

"I'm pregnant."

"Oh, my God. Are you sure?"

"Yes."

"Do you need money?"

Penelope looks at her with puzzlement.

"For the abortion, I mean. I know Colin doesn't have any."

"Caroline." Penelope holds up a hand to silence her friend. "It was not Colin, and there is not going to be an abortion."

"What do you mean?"

"Just that, it wasn't Colin. It was Greg Neals."

"It was?"

Penelope nods.

"I, I meant, why no abortion? You can't be that far along."

Suddenly Penelope's head is on the table. She is crying. Caroline sits, silent and unmoving.

"Caroline, my mother is what you call a 'Right to Lifer' here in America."

"That doesn't mean you have to destroy your life."

"I hardly think having a baby means you destroy your life."

"That's why you were crying, right? Because you're so happy about the baby."

"I can't kill this baby."

"Penelope, abortion isn't murder."

Penelope gets up and pours out some tea. "I don't want to talk about this anymore."

Okay. "Is Alex giving you a hard time, too?"

"Alex doesn't know. Alex is too happy to ask why I'm such a wreck."

So it's true. Alex and Edward are an item. How sweet. "Will you tell your parents?"

"Of course," Penelope says, and for the first time really truly smiles. "And I can't wait to see my daddy's face, but I'll have it in England. The house is just sitting there—empty."

"I think you should tell Alex. If you change your mind, you could go to a really good clinic in New York."

"I won't change my mind, but I may tell Alex. I'll miss her."

"What do you mean? You're transferring?"

"No, but the Bullfoot foundation won't let me stay, I'm sure, and anyway I want to have my baby in England."

"So it can be like Graham Greene and say, *'England made me'*?"

"Precisely, darling."

There's a three-page form to fill out, but Susan just holds the pen, not writing anything. There aren't enough spaces for her middle name—Catherine—so she just doesn't bother. The man who comes out to get her is fifty or so, with glasses and white hair. He's wearing brown corduroys and a muted checkered shirt.

She sits on a blue scratchy chair and watches him swivel on a brown leather one.

He looks at her blank papers and then smiles. "So what's the problem?"

She finds, to her horror, that she cannot speak; she's about to cry. "Thanksgiving," she blurts out before the deluge.

He hands her a gold box of Kleenex. "It's okay," he says. "Just talk, tell me."

She does. Her mother, her mother's lover, Alexandria, Edward, the Amazon Club, her father, and the problem of where to go for Thanksgiving.

"Do you have to go anywhere?" he asks.

"What do you mean?"

"I think if you stayed here, you wouldn't die, right?"

"Right," she says very tentatively.

"You see, Susan, I think you're afraid to make a decision about where to go because you think you'll be making a decision about life-styles."

"You mean about whether I'm a lesbian or straight?"

"Right."

"But what happens at Christmas?"

"Maybe by then you'll realize that where you go has nothing to do with your sex life."

"Oh."

"Susan?" The doctor does one last final swivel. "How much do you weigh?"

"I don't know. One ten, one twelve."

"I see. Do you like the way you look?"

"Me? I think I look like a, a, I don't look like anything. I just am."

"I see. What does Alexandria look like?"

"Alex? Well, she has five earrings, she talks very fast, she's from New York, she writes for the paper, she—"

"Susan, you're telling me what she's like, not what she looks like."

"Oh. Sorry."

"No need, just try and tell me what she's like physically."

Susan leans her head back and closes her eyes. "She's very tall."

"What, seven feet?"

"No. No, I guess five ten."

"And?"

"She has a small nose, longish hair, that kind of in-between stage you know when it's not really finished?"

"Yes, go on. How about her body?"

"Well, she's kind of thin, not skinny like me, and she has a bust, but no hips and a nice ass, I guess. I've never really thought about it."

"Do you like the way she looks?"

Susan laughs. "Excuse me," she says, "but why do you think I'm here?"

"Okay. I guess I mean, would you want to look like her?"

"Oh, sure. Of course."

"Of course?"

"She's beautiful."

"Do you mean physically or as a person?"

"I don't know. Is there a difference?"

"What I'm trying to establish, Susan, is whether in wanting to make love to Alexandria you aren't projecting a desire to look like her, and an unhappiness with your own looks."

"Oh. That would make it easier, wouldn't it?"

"That all depends."

"What I mean is, if I might get home for Christmas."

He laughs, she doesn't. She would like another piece of fruitcake.

♦ ♦ ♦

"Are you insane?"

"No, Alex. Pregnant."

The salad bar against the wall glistens, and there is a clean Formica smell in the air. The sun pours in through the glass walls.

Alex lowers her voice. "I think you could have found a better place than the Looking Glass Café to tell me."

"Where? The morgue?"

"I don't know. Penelope, I don't think you can make a decision like this yourself. You need to talk to someone."

Penelope exhales some smoke. "I'll need to give these up soon. I thought I was. Talking, I mean."

Alex shakes her head. "I'm not qualified. I think you need professional help."

"I'll get it, in London at the National Health Service."

"I mean psychiatric."

"Alex, the baby's not going to come out of my head."

"This is just a big deal. A baby. Who'll raise it?"

"Me."

"On what?"

"My trust fund."

Despite herself, Alex laughs. "Got an answer for it all."

"Yes."

"What about the father?"

"Screw him."

"No, thanks."

"Look, Alex. I think no father is better than a randy father."

"I think no baby is best of all."

"I'm going to miss you, Alexandria Rust. You drive me insane, but I love you."

"Don't do it, Penelope, I can't bear it here, not alone."

"You've got Edward now."

Edward, yes, well. "No man can ever replace an Amazon, Penelope, you know that."

"Yes, yes, I do."

"Will you stick it out for the rest of the semester?"

"No, I think I'll just fly out over the Thanksgiving holidays. No fuss or bother. Come with me as far as New York?"

"Edward and I were going to stay in Chapel Hill."

"Oh."

"Yes, oh."

"So you've crossed that hurdle."

Funny, that she should ever have thought it was such a big deal. Now that she wants to do it and knows who she is doing it with, sex has become something she can talk about, think about, and do with relative ease and no pain. "Yes, I guess I have."

"He always did like pretty girls."

"Oh, Penelope." Alex begins to cry. "I guess you'll be a pretty mother now."

"Yes. Maybe Daddy can find me a career diplomat, and I won't have to worry about that anymore. And baby makes three." Penelope laughs shortly. "I wasn't doing so hot solo," she whispers.

"You were perfect, Penelope, always perfect to me."

"Check," says Penelope.

"Penelope, if I went with you to New York, would you think about an abortion? I could take care of you, and we could go to a safe, discreet clinic. Please, Penelope, this is one time you can't do something to get your dad's attention. This involves another person. A baby."

"How do you know I don't want the baby?"

"I'm guessing that if it were something you were really

sure of, you wouldn't have asked me to lunch to discuss it. You just would have told me."

"Well, there's some truth to that."

"Penelope, I'm not asking for a complete yes or no. Just come to New York."

"And get an abortion?"

"Well, yes. Get an abortion. Penelope, you're twenty years old. What are you going to do with a baby?"

"Won't Edward mind?"

Alex is so relieved she almost cries. "No. No. Come on, let's go buy your ticket."

18.

New York in November

At the Rust house, Thanksgiving is never a big deal. Between Alex's diet mania, her sister Nicole's disdain for any kind of poultry, and Dr. Rust's lack of culinary talent, the family is lucky even to get fed.

"Well, thank God Penelope's missed so many Thanksgivings being abroad, is all I have to say. She hasn't any idea how badly I'm doing." Dr. Rust looks up from her magazine and glances at her daughter, who is lying sprawled across the couch. "I still think you might have let me know earlier, Alex. I had to air out the guest room and change the sheets in between rounds. I hope she doesn't notice the dirt on the floor."

"She won't, but please don't let her know she's put you out any. She'll get on the next plane home."

"Alexandria, now be truthful, which one of you needs the abortion?"

"Mom, for crying out loud, she does. I wouldn't have bothered you if it were just me. But Penelope's nervous."

"No need. I fixed everything up with June." June is one of Dr. Rust's colleagues; they are both attending doctors at St. Luke's. Dr. Rust is a cancerous cells specialist, June an OBGYN.

"Maybe I'll take her to see a movie."

"A movie? Why don't you go for a walk? It's very mild out, and everything has that wonderful pre-Christmas look."

"Mom, New York has a pre-Christmas look starting at Halloween."

"I know that, dear, but Penelope doesn't. Go and get her. I think she's in Nicole's room using the stereo."

Before she knocks on the door and enters, Alex can hear strains of "In the Name of Love" by U2. Penelope is lying on Nicole's bed holding a Raggedy Ann that used to belong to Alex. She has been crying.

"Penelope, what is it? Everything's going to be okay, I promise."

"I always thought that when I had a baby it would be the result of this overwhelming, frightening love. It didn't take any love to sleep with Greg."

Until this moment Alex assumed that Colin had recanted. Greg, Greg Neals, she thinks. Well, that makes more sense. "Penelope," she says, turning to the problem at hand, "you're not going to have this baby. The baby you do have will be the product of love. It's waiting for you."

"What if I used up the egg that would have been my perfect baby on this one, and then I kill it?"

"A baby isn't perfect because of the egg, but how it's brought up. No baby brought up by a twenty-year-old and a trust fund can be the baby you want."

"I know, but..." Penelope sits up and hands the soggy doll to Alex. "I'm starving."

"Good. Let's go out for a walk and scrounge up some food."

"Okay, pass me my sweater."

At the front door, Mr. Rust hands each girl twenty dollars and says, "Don't stay out too late, Alexandria."

Alex starts to correct him and decides it's just not worth it.

Once on the street Penelope lights a cigarette and, throwing down the match, asks, "When did you switch to Alex?"

"After the rape."

"Don't you think you could switch back, now that you have Edward and all?"

"I don't have Edward, and dating him doesn't make me pretty."

"Funny, Caroline thought it did. And I always judge pretty by men."

"I always thought I did, too. Susan was pretty, therefore Edward wanted her. Caroline was an aberration. I guess I haven't figured out which rule I follow."

"There aren't any rules, Alex."

"Aren't there?"

"No."

"Oh."

◆ ◆ ◆

Lincoln Center is deserted, the fountain dry, all the pretty people inside watching the holiday matinee opera or ballet. Both girls stretch out on the black marble rim of the fountain. They stare at the sky awhile, silent until Alex says, "I am so full."

"Wait until tomorrow; we can puke in harmony."

"I don't do it anymore."

"Really? How come?"

"You have to really want to get it out of you, be obsessed."

"I am not obsessed to have this baby out," Penelope says. Alex is silent. Maybe Penelope is just thinking aloud.

"Did I ever tell you about my sister Francesca, the youngest?" Penelope asks.

"I thought you were the baby."

"Well, technically, I am. Francesca was never born."

Alex sits up, dangling her legs inside the parched, dusty marble. "Come again?"

"Daddy made Mum get rid of it."

"What do you mean, 'made' her?"

"Just that. He told her to get rid of the baby or he'd chuck her out."

Alex has heard plenty about Mr. Samms, but it is rare that Penelope mentions her mother. "How do you know?" she asks carefully, not wanting to change Penelope's focus to tomorrow's event.

"I listened at the library door, darling. The baby was fathered by me dad's effeminate-looking secretary, whom I lusted after for two years and who was fired before Francesca was aborted."

"Are you sure it was a girl?" Alex is aware of the danger

of this conversation; she can hear, hovering in the wings, the shadow of Penelope's own abortion, but she is at a loss on how to keep it at bay.

"No. But Mummy was and called her Francesca, after Francis, Daddy's secretary. She did it just to get under his skin. It was supposed to be this big secret, but we all knew, even the boys. And of course every morning until D-Day, she'd start breakfast saying, "Francesca and I slept well last night, did you?" And then she'd smile this big vicious smile at Daddy, and he'd turn purple, a better color than the time I said I might be a bastard. I really hated her then."

"I can imagine."

"Can you?" Penelope rolls onto her stomach. "I doubt it. It doesn't bother you that your father can't remember to call you Alex."

"Yes, it does."

"No, not really. You see, if it were me and my dad, I'd take a dirty tampon and write Alex all over his study walls."

"Ugh, Penelope, that's disgusting. You're gross."

"Gross, but effective." Effective. Bullshit, she has yet to be effective on the vacuum king, on anything, and she is not going to let someone take this chance away from her. She sits up suddenly, shaking out her short hair.

"I'm sorry, Alex, I can't do it. I'm going home tomorrow."

"Penelope, it's all arranged." The lameness of this rings in Alex's ears, and the erect figure of her friend tells her she has lost.

"Unarrange it."

Alex crosses and uncrosses her legs. They look pretty thin to her—tonight. She tugs at an earring. Who gives a fuck what her legs look like; their size will execute no magic hold on Penelope.

"I'm going home. And if it's a boy, I'll name it Francis."

"And if it's a girl?"

"Francesca. Francesca Alexandria. And she'll be pretty enough to rate Alexandria." Penelope looks over at Alex. She can see some gold glowing through Alex's hair, which is falling totally over her face. "Like you are. You are pretty enough to rate Alexandria, and I love you and will miss you."

Alex begins to cry, ugly tears that contort her face. "I want you to be always happy," she gasps out.

Dusk has settled in and around the glass windows of Lincoln Center. Penelope gathers Alex in her arms. "I'm having a baby, Alexandria, not disappearing from life. Not your life or my life. I'm going off to make my life happier."

"I know you believe that. I'm just so scared for you." Alex has stopped crying. "Can you afford the airfare home?"

"Sensible to the end, aren't you, darling? Well, yes, I have an American Express card on my father's account for emergencies."

Alex laughs. "I guess this rates."

"I think so." Penelope stretches back on the fountain. She pats her abdomen. "Francesca," she murmurs. "Francesca, Francis, Francesca."

19.

When She Leaves

Alex and Edward take the same flight back to Chapel Hill. He tells her he got no work done, he missed her too much, that they should have tried to get together. She tells him Penelope is leaving and why. She does not say, "I missed you, also." Does not think it. If he notices, he does not remark upon it.

"I'm sorry. I know how you'll miss her."

"No. You can't possibly imagine. This is like Celia dying, only I keep thinking that if I had been smart enough, I could have found a way to keep Penelope here."

"Alex, not being smart enough has never been your problem. Maybe she wants the baby."

"Don't be ridiculous. No thinking twenty-year-old female wants a baby."

"All right. Maybe you just think too much."

She turns her face to the window and wonders if the batteries in Penelope's Walkman will last the trip to London.

"I saw all the guys from my high school soccer team. We went back to the West End for drinks. That place hasn't changed a bit."

"Nicole and her friends go there now."

"Steve really likes Yale."

"Does he?" Alex had met Steve at parties in high school. She is sure he is the one who called her tight-assed.

"He couldn't believe we were dating. He told me that you take the valedictorian to lunch, not to bed." Edward runs his hand up Alex's leg.

She smiles. "I remember Penelope saying that she had been out to lunch so many times that she was going to die if she didn't get a dinner date."

They take a cab into Chapel Hill, and Alex says, "It's funny. Last year Penelope and Caroline came to pick me up from the airport after Thanksgiving. I'm not even sure where Caroline went this weekend."

Edward makes no comment. They stop at her place first.

"I'll call you later," he says, helping take her bags to the apartment door.

"I'm moving into Penelope's old room," she says.

"You told me that already."

"Bye."

"I'll call you."

Alex does not think that she has heard this line before, but that this time she knows he will, and how nice it is not to have to worry about it. Then she takes a deep breath and wonders how she will break the news of her sudden departure to Cristen.

In the small house on Carr Street, Alex does not sleep. She should be bone-tired, for she is running a lot and studying very hard. She paces the floor, looking at the Rolling Stones' poster and Penelope's collage. There is a huge void in Alex, the kind she used to fill with food, but she knows that all the food in the world won't bring Penelope back to her. She packs up all of Penelope's clothes. It occurs to Alex that the miniskirts and halter tops will be of no use to her friend, but she folds them neatly into brown cardboard boxes anyway. She recognizes several outfits as ones bought on trips to the mall and wonders if she will ever follow behind Penelope again, watching her pick, select, discard. What will I do if Edward takes me to a party? Who will dress me, do my hair, choose my earrings? Who will help me study, decide on a major? The answer is clear. No one. All she has left is Edward, and that is not always easy. Last night, after she asked him to leave, he shouted at her, "There's me! I know you're sad, but I'm still here. I love you." He just didn't get it. She had work to do. A lot of work. He can be a darling, though. He has offered to drive her to the post office.

"Stay in the car, no point in you standing on line, too," he tells her. "I'll take them in."

"Be careful with that, those are her records."

"Okay."

"She told me to keep her earrings. But I'm sending them back."

"Well, that's okay, you've got enough earrings."

Alex looks at him sharply. "What does that mean?"

"What do you think?"

"I don't know. Suppose you tell me what you mean."

"Nothing."

"I think a pregnant woman should wear a lot of jewelry."

"I guess it distracts from her waist," Edward says, unloading the last box.

"Why should she want to?"

"Forget it," he says lamely.

"Jeez, you're articulate today," Alex says.

"I won't be too long with this stuff."

The post office parking lot is deserted, and Alex watches Edward through the windowpane and glass front doors of the post office. He looks all warped out of shape. His height and thinness are ridiculously exaggerated, and for just a moment she sees him through Penelope's eyes. She plays with the radio dial and the heating system. She pulls out the lighter and looks at the pale gold metal coils. When he returns to the car Alex has her own eyes back again, and she smiles at him.

"You want me to take you to a movie this weekend?" he asks. "Take your mind off things."

"Well, that would be nice. I think *Yentl* is playing in Durham. I'd like to see that."

"I hate Barbra Streisand."

"Why am I not surprised?"

"Alex, let's not get in a fight."

"No. Let's not. Let's go to *Yentl* instead."

He starts the car. Laughs. Says, "Oh, for the days of 'you decide.'"

Caroline has returned to college life. She will need good grades to transfer, and she begins to go to classes and the library. When she runs into Alex in the Pit, it is a little awkward. Alex tells her of Penelope's departure.

"Well, I thought she would. Did I tell you I was transferring?"

"Why?"

Because I couldn't stand the sight of the two of you. Two proud Amazons slowly closing the door on me. And now I can't stand the sight of you and Edward. "Because I'm unhappy."

"Oh, Caroline, I'm sorry. I haven't really been here for you, have I?"

Caroline shrugs. She does not want to take the hand Alex is reaching out. It's too late. Alex has too much already.

"I miss playing scrutiny," Alex says suddenly.

"I was never very good at it," Caroline says. "I don't drink Tab." She walks away from her friend toward the library, wishing they could sit on the steps together, pretend they were roommates and that this semester had never happened.

Susan is sitting in the library's reading room at one of the wooden tables with gold electric lights. This is the only room she can work in without getting claustrophobic. The stacks make neat rows around the tables, leaving some open walking space, to show off the blue carpeting. At both ends are floor-to-ceiling windows, reminding her that there is a world outside the library, motivating her to work and get out into it. She is trying to make sense of her econ. book, which she did not touch over Thanksgiving. She was too busy moping around town and eating fruitcake. She sees Edward at one of the other tables. There are papers and books spread before him. He's probably finally writing that philosophy paper he spent all semester talking about, boring her to death: the relative influences of Plato and Aristotle on the modern world. She laughs and remembers when Alex said that his concept of his own intelligence always overshot its mark. However, he is intelligent, and she has to resist the impulse to take her textbook over to him and say, "Help. Please explain." She does not know that he would be delighted to help someone, anyone. That he would feel useful again. Powerful, even. She knows only that it is too quiet to concentrate. Damn. She might fail this course. Someone slips into the empty chair at her table. It is Caroline, and Susan looks at her in surprise. She hopes Edward is watching them, worrying that they might compare notes.

"Is this what kept you here Thanksgiving?" Caroline asks, motioning to the econ. book.

Susan wonders how Caroline knows. She must have seen her around—there hadn't been that many people. "No. I just didn't want to go home."

"Funny. Me neither. I'm transferring next semester, and I don't want to get into it with my parents."

"How come you're going?"

Caroline tilts back her chair and stares out the glass wall a minute, as if she considers telling the truth. "I don't know. There just doesn't seem to be anything here for me anymore."

"Alexandria told me that Penelope left. I'm sorry about that. I really liked her."

Caroline laughs and pulls two Cokes out of her bag. "Want one?"

"Thanks."

They open them slowly, trying to cover the little hiss of the tops.

"Susan, Penelope was never anything but a bitch to you. How come you liked her?"

"I guess I didn't. It's just her going seems to have everybody down. You, Alex. I don't know. I'm sure she's nice enough, or she and Alex wouldn't have been close."

"Got a pretty high opinion of Miss Rust, don't you?"

"Well, I like her," Susan says evasively. She doesn't want to get into talking about Alexandria.

"You do? Even though she's dating Edward?"

"She said something once. That if she hated every girlfriend of an old boyfriend, she'd have no one to talk to. I guess I'm like that, too."

"Got a lot in common with her?"

"No, I guess not." I'm working on it, though.

"I like your earring."

Susan fingers her diamond stud. "Thanks."

Caroline takes a swallow of Coke.

"Caroline, would you like to come over tonight? To the house, I mean. It'll be empty, most of the girls are going to a mixer."

"Why aren't you?"

Not sure I like men anymore. "Not up to it."

"Well, sure. I can brave a sorority house, if it's empty. What time?"

"I've got a ton to do still. How about ten?"

"Sure." Caroline picks up her stuff, putting the empty can under the table. "See you."

When Susan leaves the library she goes to the cafeteria for lunch. At one of the vinyl-covered tables Alex is drinking coffee.

"Guess you're not hungry."

"I'm lonely," she says. She looks at Susan's thin face and repeats, "I'm lonely, not hungry."

"I guess you miss Penelope."

"Yes."

"I'm sorry you're upset."

Alex smiles. "Thank you. That means a lot," she says sarcastically. Alex feels very ugly at this particular moment; she doesn't want to discuss Penelope with Susan. In fact, she doesn't want to discuss anything with Susan, who is short and has a southern accent. "See you later," she says, picking up her gloves and sweater and striding out the door.

Well, Susan thinks. My problem is solved; if I do want to sleep with that bitch, she doesn't even want to talk to me, so there's no choice, is there?

"Wasn't that the best?" Alex asks, getting into the car as Edward holds the door open for her.

He walks around the back and gets in on the driver's side. "It was okay."

"Okay? Poor Barbra, she never keeps the man. Not Sharif in *Funny Girl,* not Redford in *The Way We Were,* and not Patinkin in *Yentl.* Imagine settling for Amy Irving when you could have Barbra."

"I don't need to imagine. After that loud mouth, I'd run

to Amy so fast it would make your head spin."

"Edward!"

"Well, I would. Want to fight?"

"You asked me that already."

He does not laugh, and she says, "I think you have no taste."

"That says a lot about you."

"Yeah, well, what can I say? You got lucky."

"Lucky. That's what Susan used to say. 'Every girl in the Pi Phi house says I'm excessively lucky.'"

She does not point out how tacky it is to quote old girlfriends. She says, "Edward, you just missed the turn-off. Now double back."

"Jesus, Alex. You are so bossy. You even make love in a bossy way."

"I haven't noticed that you dislike the way I make love."

He makes a U-turn.

"Edward, you really didn't like the movie?"

"Too feminist for me."

"That's a term you throw around loosely."

"What do you mean?"

"Well, for example, you consider Penelope a feminist, right?"

"All the Amazons are."

"That's not a word you can use, and I would hardly call Penelope's going home to find a husband and have a baby feminist."

"Whose baby is it, anyway? Did Colin finally surrender?"

"Whose? That's all you care about, isn't it? Whose?"

"I'm curious."

"You don't care that she's throwing away her future to have Greg Neals's baby, do you?"

"Susan once said that having a baby was the greatest honor a woman could have."

"Great thinker, that girl."

"Okay. Maybe Susan does have a 'space to let' sign, but at least you always knew what was there, even if it was air."

"That's nice if you like air."

"Alex, would you just shut up?"

"Oh, sure, of course; anything you say." Alex pauses for effect. "Dear."

They're driving up Franklin now, and before he makes the right onto Airport Road she says, "Edward, drop me on campus. There's a book in the undergrad I need."

He watches her get out of the car. She unfolds her long legs, tries to untangle her hair from her five earrings. She sees on his face the expression he has when she undresses for bed. What is your problem? she wants to ask.

"Alexandria."

She leans back into the car to get her bag.

"Yes?" Her tone implies that she couldn't give a damn about anything he ever has to say.

"Fuck you!" He slams her door shut from the inside and takes off the way he's always wanted to: burning rubber.

With her headphones on, Susan is lying on her bed listening to an old Carly Simon album. When Edward opens her door and says, not as a question but as a demand, "Let's go to bed," she's not really surprised. She just hits the lights and turns the stereo volume down.

Thank God, thank God. I can go home for Christmas.

♦ ♦ ♦

When Caroline gets to the Pi Phi house at 10:20—late because she'd been thinking about not coming—a girl wearing pearl add-a-beads directs her to Susan's room. There's no light on under the door, so Caroline knocks softly, thinking Susan might be sleeping.

"Susan?"

"That's Caroline," she hears the girl say.

"Oh, Christ." Definitely Edward.

She steps into the room and turns on the overhead. "You bastard," she says.

"Lovely to see you, too," he says.

"Where'd you leave Alex? In your bed or hers?"

"On campus."

"Caroline, don't tell her."

"Susan, you aren't worth mentioning."

Of course she finds Alex sitting on the steps staring into the deserted Pit, which is eerily illuminated by the neon yellow pouring out from both still opened libraries.

Caroline sits on the step right above Alex and puts both arms around her friend. Now, now that she's needed, she can reach out a hand, reach out a hand to a wounded warrior.

"I was just thinking of Penelope," Alex says.

"Of course."

"No, not Samms. Did you ever read the *Odyssey*?"

"Yes."

"And you remember how it took him ten years of hell to get to her, and how she waited, turning down all those suitors?"

"Yes," Caroline says softly. "Yes."

"Well, she must have been pretty for Odysseus to want

to get to her so bad, and she sure was smart to keep all those guys at bay, holding out for the real thing."

"Sure she was. You think smart pretty girls originated with you?"

"Oh, Caroline. He wanted her, though. Nowadays there are tons of Penelopes, and I can't find one Odysseus."

"Been looking ten years, Alex?"

"No. I don't believe it's worth it. Now a Penelope, that would be a find."

Caroline pictures a life where the ultimate achievement would be to find someone who mirrors yourself. What she loved about Alex and Penelope is how they matched her physically and mentally. It wasn't enough. Can she pass this knowledge on?

"I want to tell you something, Alexandria Rust."

"Yeah, what's that?"

"There are no innocent men."

"I know. I know."

"Just hang onto yourself, because I love you."

Why couldn't you have been a man?

I don't know, but I'm going to try my darnedest next time around.

Come back to me, Penelope Samms. I need you.

"He's with Susan, right?"

"He's with a pretty girl. He doesn't understand about Amazons."

"Life sucks, you know?"

"I know. I know."

The silent gray turns to black and envelopes them the way no lover can or has or will.